A. B. Seals

Rockford

A Romance

A. B. Seals

Rockford
A Romance

ISBN/EAN: 9783337351038

Printed in Europe, USA, Canada, Australia, Japan

Cover: Foto ©Andreas Hilbeck / pixelio.de

More available books at **www.hansebooks.com**

ROCKFORD.

CHAPTER I.

WE are all creatures of impulse, guided in the main by our passions, whims and caprices. The human mind is so constituted that it requires a certain quantity of aliment, like the physical system, to sustain and keep it upon its proper balance. That pabulum must be garnered from the great field of literature, which blooms and blossoms in every nation of the civilized globe. Like the pilgrim in search of Truth, the neophyte of learning is puzzled to find a shrine at which he may worship and receive the signet which will serve as a passport into the Temple of Fame. What the unhappy pilgrim had considered as Truth in his own country, was so different from that crowning virtue of mortals in other regions, that his heart sank within him, and he girded his loins afresh, rebuckled the sandals upon his weary feet, and retraced the space of his fruitless journey until the minarets and spires of his own village gladdened his eyes once more. The taste of our people is so different, that it behooves the writers of romances to introduce

scenes into their works which may please all classes of
society; even then, the more fastidious may heap coals
of fire upon the heads of the innocent authors.

True, there is a great diversity of opinion existing in
the minds of individuals, even, who are competent judges
of literature, as to what constitutes true merit. That is
just and proper. If their minds ran in the same smooth,
unruffled channel, the mass of readers would become disgusted with the easy path they tread, and retire from a
race in which there are no competitors. It is controversy
that brings truth to light, and fashions out the safest
plan for the government of all social bodies. Like the
rays of incidence and reflection, which move always in
equal angles though in different directions, the champi-
ons upon the arena of debate divest every question of
its surplus proportions, and erect a model which is
pleasing to every one; or each party creates a system
of principles which has its own admirers.

As there is a marked difference in the opinions of
wise legislators upon the systems of government, so
there is a diversity in the minds of those who write
novels, plays, and books of amusement. The works of
fiction, of late years, are masked batteries, from which
the authors assail the public in every conceivable form.
The religion of particular sects is ridiculed and put to
the blush after a style so ludicrous, that the members
are often tempted to renounce their faith and adopt
some other creed. It is not to be doubted, that the
loose writers of French romances have prepared the
way for every revolution which has deluged the streets

of Paris with blood, for the last hundred years. But scribblers will write, and even a starving population will buy and read books. If the best talent of the country is not engaged in writing histories, essays, or romances of a legitimate literary character, the legions of *small fry,* who have no higher aspirations than to amuse the giddy crowd for a brief hour, are filling our book-stores with their worthless trash, which is daily corrupting the morals of our youth, thus paving the way for the subversion and dethronement of reason.

How shall this thing be guarded against? The deplorable **system** cannot be changed, except by the force of education and right reason. Teach a boy that the unequalled romances of Walter Scott are not to be laid aside for the lascivious productions of Eugene Sue, or the startling tales of horror which have rendered Alexander Dumas so noted, and you place him in the right path to avoid insurmountable obstructions in his literary pilgrimage. The masses of mankind cannot be taught in a single day or a year; but a series of years spent by the educators of youth may effect a great change in this matter.

The appearance of so many new novels of late years from writers unknown to fame, will tempt many inexperienced authors to soar into realms of ether bright, but their own leaden weight will bring them down upon a level with terrestrial things. If a book without merit forces its way into polite circles, the eager crowd may read it; but the condemnation of wise critics will soon consign it to the shades of oblivion. Criticism is a sharp lancet which is admirably adapted to the work of draining off superfluous fountains, yet it often kills an innocent victim. The English and Scotch Reviewers sent so many shafts into the ranks of MISTAKENDOM, who were trying to force a passage into the Temple of Fame, that none but the valiant and true in the palmy days of Byron, Scott and Moore, were permitted to climb high up the hill of the Muses.

If a romance is not intended to instruct, as well as amuse the reader, it is written in vain. There are but few authors who are capable of spinning out a tale by merely giving narrations, after the pleasing style of the old class of writers, therefore a variety of characters must be introduced to cater to the taste of the multitude. The monotone of a reader renders his hearers weary and uneasy; yet the musical modulations of a well-trained voice fall upon the attentive ears of an eager auditory like the thrilling chimes of a golden bell. The description of a beautiful landscape would not be so charming if the writer should draw the picture of no rugged mountains and desolate heaths. A beautiful, clear rippling brook, as it rushes heedlessly and playfully along over its pebbly bed, gladdens the eye and freshens the grove; but the very flocks and herds loathe and fly from a sluggish, turbid pool. It is contrast that renders beauty more sublime, and variety scatters all the flowers of the forest in our paths; even the kingdom of Flora would bloom in vain if the hedges were planted alone with roses or lilies. The sensitive plant, which shrinks from the touch and closes its tiny leaves when the rough winds visit them too freely, has no sweet flower, but every model of grace and beauty exists in its slender form. It is not to be excluded from the garden, for it is a sweet sister to the flowers. They look more beautiful by its side, and they protect and guard it from harm.

I propose to write a novel, not after the style of trashy authors, whose existence is only ephemeral, but one which may interest and instruct the reader. The abuse of no religious sect will find a place in these pages. If the work has merit, the public will soon discover it: if it has none, it will share the fate of thousands of others which were written only to gratify the whim of the authors. Like the author of Gil Blas, I respectfully ask a perusal of this work. The reader may remember the fable that the author relates in the opening chapter of that masterly work.

CHAPTER II.

"THE moon shines so brightly, my dear," said Mr. Rockford to his wife, as he made preparations for an evening walk, "that I have an inclination to step over to the village hotel and spend an hour in conversation with our friends."

"Look! Mr. Rockford, how the baby smiles upon you. Do you not hear him say, 'Papa'? He extends his little hands for you to take him. Do remain with us this beautiful Winter evening. There is such a pleasant. bright fire burning in the grate, and the hall looks so comfortable."

Mr. Rockford excused himself, and promising to return by ten o'clock, hurried from the house, and was soon walking briskly in the direction of the principal square of the town. Mrs. Rockford kissed the rosy cheeks of Sebastian more than once, and standing him upon the marble slab which supported a costly mirror, she pressed her darling to her bosom as he endeavored to strike his own beautiful image reflected from the crystal surface of the glass. Sebastian was a promising little boy of two years of age. His light auburn ringlets clustered in many a curl about his well shaped head. His blue eyes made his mother glad, when they beamed upon her with an expression of intelligence so far beyond one of his age.

"Bless mother's little darling; she would not take the world for him. Kiss mother, and then get down upon the carpet and play with Jupe."

(Jupe was a little white woolly fice, which had been so much petted, that he considered no place about the house too sacred for him to enter.) The sofa and rocking-chairs were occupied by this diminutive specimen of the canine race, whenever it pleased him to take a nap. Jupe was never satisfied when little Sebastian was out of his sight. Sebastian returned his love with all the ardor that an affectionate child is capable of possessing. When Jupe would play too freely with Sebastian's toys. or throw down his block houses and run off with his ivory rattle, the boy would chase and fleck him with his whip. Jupe had too much sense or did not care to hurt Sebastian; but as dogs are not more patient of ill treatment than human beings are, Jupe became nervous when Sebastian bit his soft velvet ears too hard, and never failed to give him an unlucky snap upon the fingers. Sebastian would run to his mother, crying, with many bitter complaints against Jupe. She, upon occasions of that kind, would order Jupe to be moderately chastised, and sent to his kennel in disgrace.

"Here, Jupe," said Mrs. Rockford, as she stood Sebastian down upon the floor, "come and play with darling."

Jupe barked immoderately, and playfully bit Sebastian upon his leg. They were soon rolling over and over upon the floor, while Mrs. Rockford beheld the scene with much delight. Her happiness seemed to be concentrated in the boundless love she entertained for her son. She almost idolized him, and yet her love for her husband was not in the least diminished by its being divided with Sebastian. All the wealth of Golconda, added to the priceless pearls of the ocean, are not so dear in a parent's eyes as a lovely child. Thus thought Mrs. Rockford, as she seated herself before the glowing grate, with the household pets playing at her feet. She was a lovely woman, capable of rendering a household happy and sharing the felicity herself. She was industrious and prided herself in arranging and putting every thing in its proper place. The piano was dressed off with a costly covering, embroidered by her own fingers. A green vine formed the border of this magnificent piece of her handiwork. In the center was a vase of flowers, and numerous devices filled the space. The embroidered mats for the lamps were not the least attractive ornaments of the center-table, and the willow basket, filled with Sebastian's toys, was beautified with numerous emblems wrought in crewel. These were only a few of the fruits of her accomplishments and industry.

It is generally supposed that women are unhappy because the greater portion of their time is spent within doors, but such is not the case. They have a thousand things to interest them which are not attractive to men. A woman will sit for weeks, and labor with her needle, embroidering a pair of undersleeves or a single cambric handkerchief. When Mrs. Rockford was not employing her time in reading, or playing with Sebastian, it was thus that she amused herself. She rang a little brazen bell that lay upon the mantel, and Lucinda, the housemaid, entered. Lucinda brought the work-basket, which was filled with the scraps of many samples of domestic goods. Placing the basket by her side, this industrious lady commenced selecting some of the latest styles which were to form the squares of a quilt for Sebastian's bed. Being satisfied with the selection of colors, she commenced cutting the pieces into diminutive squares, triangles and crescents. If the manufacture of quilts is considered a waste of time, it is truly a great saving of rags. It would be but light employment, indeed, for a lady to make enough quilts for a whole community, if it were only requisite for her to cut the different goods into pieces of the length of the quilts, and sew them together. The good ladies ought to have their own way about their household affairs. Let them cut their cloth into as many fairy-like sections as they please, and stitch in rose, lily or japonica patterns.

But Sebastian was not of this opinion, nor was Jupe, or at least their actions indicated it, for they rose from the floor as if by mutual consent, and made an attack upon the good lady's basket. The boy emptied it upon the floor and commenced selecting the scraps of the brightest colors, before his mother was aware of his intentions. Jupe seized several bits of cloth, regardless of their whiteness, with his tiny sharp teeth, and ran to his usual safe retreat under the sofa. He was so fairy-like in his physical proportions, that he could occupy a very small space. Lucinda had upon several occasions tried to eject him from his lurking place. The sofa was so shaped that its frame work almost rested upon the floor. Jupe effected his entrance to this safe asylum by a small aperture between one of the legs and slabs of the sofa. It was necessary to remove the sofa in order to arrest the miscreant. Jupe had sense enough to know this; besides he was all pluck, and if he took it into his head to withstand a siege he would maintain his position and remain in his impregnable fortress from the rising of the sun to the going down thereof. (Sebastian ran all over the room, scattering his trophies, while Jupe applauded him by keeping up a continual barking.

Lucinda was ordered to gather up the scraps, and place them beyond the reach of Sebastian. The servant did as she was directed, and Sebastian was upon the eve of receiving a slight chastisement for his conduct, when his mother remembered that he would relate everything to his father when he came home. Mr. Rockford was not favorable to the rigid training of children, believing that a child should be taught the enormity of an offence before the punishment is inflicted. The mother laid aside her work for the balance of the evening, and ordered her basket put away. She was in no mood to proceed with her work, nor could she have done so to advantage, for Jupe had some of her select scraps in his safe keeping. She knew he would stay under the sofa for hours to come. The war had been waged, and he was not yet willing to surrender. Mrs. Rockford readily forgave her child, but poor Jupe must suffer in the flesh when she should lay her hands upon him. She smoothed the dishevelled ringlets of her darling, kissed his coral lips, and took him in her arms and sang him to sleep.

How blessed is that happy mother who has an angel sleeping in her arms! An innocent child is the true type of those celestial beings, whose dwelling place is Paradise. If a child has the germs of sin within it, the commencement of its trangressions is not co-eval with its birth. (Angels guard the slumbers of infants, and fan their cheeks with snow white wings.) Sebastian slept the sweet sleep of happy childhood. His mother unloosed his tiny fingers from her neck, around which his arms had clung as if for protection, and gently placing him in his little bed, covered him up carefully. Taking a book from the center-table, she sat down to read until the return of her husband.

When Mr. Rockford left his stately mansion to walk to the town, the moon shone brilliantly and the pebbly walks resounded beneath his manly tread. The steeples of the churches and the dome of the town hall reflected the silvery rays of the orb of night from their metallic coverings. Crofton was a quiet, nice town, and possessed an intelligent population, noted for integrity, sobriety and industry. In the business season the place had a bustling, commercial-like appearance. It was a seaport whose harbor admitted ships of light tonnage. Situated at the mouth of a navigable river, which had its source in the upland districts of the State, the commodious ware-rooms were the recipients of the staple produce of the country. Besides, the place was considered very healthy, and was frequently resorted to by those in search of a quiet retreat. The waves of the Atlantic dashed against the base of the steep bluff upon which the town stood, and the ears of the citizens had learned to love the harmonious echoes of the moving billows.

Mr. Rockford approached the square upon which the principal hotel was located, and was proceeding quietly along the walk when his attention was arrested by the appearance of a large crowd assembled at the corners of the street. He approached the assemblage and enquired the cause of the excitement. One of the citizens told him that a murder had just been committed by a desperate character, and one of the most inoffensive, upright men in Crofton was the unfortunate victim. The citizens had assembled for the purpose of considering the propriety of taking the law in their own hands, and dealing out summary punishment to the offender.

Mr. Rockford was a good man, and having practiced law in Crofton many years, his views upon all subjects were duly respected. He was instantly importuned by those present, to speak to the infuriated citizens, and, if possible, to induce them to respect the supremacy of the law. He responded to their call, and mounting the steps of one of the stores, admonished them not to abuse the privileges they then enjoyed as law-abiding and God-fearing men. He said it was true that one of the best men in the community had fallen by the hands of a desperate man, yet he was in safe custody, and they had laws which ought truly to be executed; but the Statutes of the State pointed out the plan by which they should be enforced.

The citizens were induced to pursue the course pointed out by Mr. Rockford, and the assembly adjourned to the Court House, where the case was legally disposed of. The jury of inquest having made up their verdict against the prisoner, the proof before the Court was conclusive, after the examination of three witnesses. The prisoner was sent to jail under the charge of murder. Mr. Rockford sought his peaceful and happy home, rejoicing that he had been the instrument of preserving his community from the stigma of a desperate act about to be committed by the irated, but well meaning citizens.

CHAPTER III.

IT was a custom indulged in by Sir Walter Scott to rise early and take long morning walks while he was engaged in the composition of any one of his great works. He supposed that his mind was free from care at such times, and his solitary rambles lent that beauty and vigor to his compositions which are seen in the writings of no other authors. The human mind is so constituted that it requires rest, exercise, and indulgence. Being a philosopher by nature, this great man knew that the mind, like the body, would be exposed to the ravages of decay, without fresh pabulum to feed upon. He would stand for hours and indulge his fancy in beholding the silvery sheets of water pour over the rough ledges of rock, and unite again in the bosom of the soft rippling stream. Coleridge composed the "Rime of the Ancient Mariner" during a pleasant evening excursion. Lord Byron would never have written the unequalled poem of "Childe Harold," if his footsteps had never wandered beyond the limits of his native country. As sweetly as his liquid verse flows in melodious streams, he confessed that it was quite difficult for him to compose, unless he was very familiar with his subject, and at such times as his mind was completely under his control. Shelley had a peculiar

fancy for sail boats. If he was not indulging his fondness for this sport in sailing across the lake, he would,
when fatigued with labor, hasten to the water side, and,
child-like, sail diminutive boats near the shore. It is
related of him, that he was so fond of constructing
ships and sail boats out of paper, that he would tear
leaves from a book however so costly. Upon one occasion, he was sitting upon the banks of a river in a
meditative mood. He had left his little boats at home,
and, unfortunately, had no book with him. He could
not be deprived of his pleasure, and taking out a Bank
bill of considerable value, he fashioned out a boat and
flung it into the stream.

Napoleon Bonaparte so prepared his mind for labor by
by violent exercise, that he accomplished more in a given
space than any General of modern times. And if we
except Julius Cæsar, who was one of the most accomplished scholars among the ancients, the great Napoleon
had no superior. The periods of history are so strangely
divided by those who are considered competent judges.
that we are in doubt whether it is proper to class Julius
Cæsar among the ancients, or not. Some authors facetiously speak of events which happened before antiquity
itself began; but let dates begin or end as the caprices
of men may limit them, Julius Cæsar finished the ancient and laid the corner-stone of modern times. His
history of the Gallic War was composed in his camps :
it could not have been written by one, with half the
vigor, who was not a participator himself in those interesting scenes.

2

Josephus Napoleon Bonaparte Snibbens had a great fancy for imitating distinguished men. He imagined that he was learned, for the reason that he had read and studied the works of great authors. It was certain that he had read "Robbins' Outlines of History" and "Tooke's Pantheon." He could discourse eloquently upon the mighty deeds of the Egyptian heroes; and when he was relating the scenes of the Chinese revolution he always grew pathetic. Mr. Snibbens was a great man, as most of his patrons and pupils thought. He had come to Crofton to teach the juvenile portion of the community, not only the theories of the learned authors, but he intended that the society of the place should be improved by his illustrious example.

Early on the morning subsequent to the events related in the preceding chapter, Mr. Snibbens emerged from his boarding-house for the express purpose of taking his usual morning walk. The weather was cool and bracing, and the white frost glittered upon the ground like transparent crystals. Buttoning his overcoat up to his chin, and straightening up the collar to protect his ears from the cold, this modern genius directed his footsteps to the sea-side. He had not proceeded far when he met John Simpkins, one of the town merchants, on his way to his place of business.

"Good morning, friend Simpkins," said Snibbens, as he halted for a regular chat, "this is delightful weather. Thomson gives such glowing descriptions of Winter mornings, in his poem on the Seasons, that I am almost tempted to rehearse a few of the stanzas for your especial benefit."

"Ah! Mr. Snibbens," replied Simpkins, "you men of learning are excellent companions: but a plodding merchant. like myself, is always at a loss to find suitable words to repay you for your fine display of rhetoric."

Snibbens received the compliment with studied affectation, and taking a pinch of snuff, described a geometrical figure upon the ground with his walking stick, and was on the point of entering upon a discussion concerning the properties of angles, but he was so anxious to learn the particulars of the murder that he changed his determination.

"Come, friend Simpkins," said the erudite pedagogue. "please relate to me what information you have gathered relative to the heart-rending occurrence of last evening. which, as I have been informed, has no parallel in the history of Crofton." (Here Snibbens took snuff a second time, and looked wise.)

"It is true," replied Simpkins, "that it is a deed which makes one shudder to think of, yet I have read of crimes as equally horrible. Carl Royston has been the terror of this community ever since his dissipation commenced. A few years since he was an accomplished clerk in one of the principal business houses in this town. He was admired and respected by all who knew him, and was considered by his employers as a man of strict integrity. For a long time he has led a desperate life. He was supposed to have been implicated in a murder committed only a few miles from Crofton. but sufficient evidence was not produced upon the investigation to convict him. Last night he was creating a disturbance in the sitting room of the hotel, where several gentlemen were conversing, when they endeavored to pacify him. He commenced throwing the chairs about the room, and one of them struck Jonathan Winslow. That gentleman remarked that he was a peaceable man, but was not in the least inclined to submit to a wanton insult. He made no advance upon Royston, but cautioned him not to molest him again. Royston drew out a pistol and discharged its contents in the breast of Winslow, who fell and expired in a few minutes."

Mr. Simpkins wished Snibbens a very good morning, and hurried to his store. Snibbens walked down to the wharf, made a forcible speech to the waves, snuffed the sea breeze a few minutes, and retraced his steps to his boarding-house. When he entered the hall, the jingling sound of a hand-bell announced that breakfast was ready. He was a punctual man in all the relations of life, but more especially in his attendance at his meals. He took his accustomed place that morning, if not with a light heart, at least with a keen appetite.

Samuel Culverhouse, and his tidy wife, subsisted upon the profits of entertaining a dozen boarders. Mrs. Culverhouse wore a Swiss muslin cap, bordered with wide edging of her own knitting. The good dame had a pair of old-fashioned silver spectacles which had been the property of her grand-mother. The glasses were circular, and when she put them on and seated herself beside the coffee urn, she presented a very ludicrous appearance. Samuel was dressed in his everlasting suit of blue jeans, which his darling Dorothy had spun and woven with her own hands.

"Take a bit of this steak, Mr. Snibbens? fine steak —tender steak. I selected it myself," said Samuel, as he helped each one of the boarders to a portion of the savory dish.

"Mr. Snibbens, will you have cream and sugar in your coffee this morning?" said Dorothy.

"If you please, madam," said the learned pedagogue.

"Will you have much sugar in it, Mr. Snibbens?" continued the good dame.

"I am not at all particular, my dear Mrs. Culver-house," anxiously replied Snibbens, who had given the identical answers to the same queries every morning, for three years, in which he had sojourned in the house of that most excellent woman.

The conversation naturally turned upon the murder of Jonathan Winslow. Each one had a good word to say concerning the lamented man, while they all loathed the very name of Royston. Samuel entertained the opinion that there would be but little difficulty in the conviction of Royston, when the case should come up for trial. Many murderers had been turned loose upon that community, he said, because the lawyers had been ably feed; and in some instances the jury had been bribed. Samuel was not certain of this, but he was sustained by the boarders, who were not in the habit of differing materially from the opinions as expressed by the worthy host.

"I knew Winslow well, sir—knew him well," said the

hearty Samuel, as he emptied his fourth cup of coffee, and helped himself to a fresh supply of buck-wheat cakes. "A nobler man was never an inhabitant of Crofton than he was. I learn that old Mr. Winslow has employed lawyer Rockford to prosecute the case, and if he does his duty and brings the powers of his mind to act with their accustomed vigor, it is not to be doubted, but that the prisoner will be convicted."

"Samuel, my darling," said the good house-wife, raising her massive spectacles from her long Roman nose and resting them upon the frill of her muslin cap, "is it the same young Mr. Winslow who used to drive that dapple horse by here last Summer?"

"You are right, my dear," said the affectionate Samuel. "You are seldom wrong in your surmises, Dorothy. Mrs. Primrose never made the Vicar of Wakefield a better spouse than you have been to me. Have Edith to bring in some warm cakes from the kitchen."

Samuel knew exactly how to cater to the vanity of Dorothy. She returned his compliment with becoming modesty, but chided him for being so affectionate before company.

"Why, la! Samuel, what a plain spoken man you are! You will make Mr. Snibbens and Miss Jerusha Smith blush, if you do not quit using such honeyful words to me before them. I asked you a question about Mr. Winslow, and you gave me only a half an answer, and wound up by making an appeal for warm cakes."

"Just so my, dear. 'Variety is the spice of life,' and cakes are the staff of life; and you will please have my request complied with."

The good Dorothy had sent Edith to the kitchen, to assist the cook in preparing sausages for the second table, and not desiring to interfere with her own arrangements, she took a dish and tripped off to do the behests of her husband. During her absence, Mr. Snibbens related his morning's adventures, and expatiated upon the many happy thoughts that arise in the mind while the body is moderately exercised by a pleasant ramble. He never forgot to relate, in speaking of the benefits the mind derives from exercise, that Napoleon Bonaparte unloosed the leaden fetters from his mind, by walking for hours before the camp-fires upon the eve of a great battle. Mr. Snibbens had read a pictorial history of the French Revolution.

The mistress of the house having made a successful trip to the kitchen, returned laden with some brown cakes spread with Goshen butter. The boarders finished a pleasant meal, and left the host and his spouse to discuss their plans for the day.

Snibbens went into the hall, sat a few minutes by the fire, picked his teeth and smoked a cigar. When the hour for opening school arrived, he went to his chamber and collected his books which he used at recitations. He placed a Key to Algebra in one pocket and a Diamond interlinear translation of Virgil in the other. Those were the best friends this noted teacher had in the world, as he overcame many obstructions by making drafts upon their oracular leaves. He went to his school-room, and rang the bell. The boys took their seats and applied themselves to their lessons.

When the class in Virgil was called up to recitation, three boys sauntered to the stand, each one carrying a dilapidated edition of the works of the Roman bard in one hand and a Latin Dictionary in the other.

"Which is the lesson, James Jones?" asked the learned teacher.

"It commences at the two hundred and fiftieth line, second Book of the Æneid, sir."

"You may commence, James," said Snibbens.

James took his sweet gum from his mouth and lent it to the boy who sat next to him, and began his recitation:

"*Vertitur interea coelum*—the interior of the heaven was inverted; *et ruit Oceano nox*—and the ocean rushed on to the night; *Involens umbra magna terramque polumque*—overturning the great shade of the earth with a pole; *Myrmidonum que dolos*—with the Myrmidonian dollars. This translation did not exactly suit Snibbens, though he supposed that the boy was not far from being right.

"Wait a moment, James, until I go into the apparatus room. I thought I heard something fall."

Snibbens went into the little room, and drawing out his translation, hastily looked over the passage which James had just read. He placed some of the retorts upon different shelves, made a noise, as if picking up something from the floor, and having arranged what the class had supposed was blown down by the wind, he returned and required James to translate the sentence again. The teacher grew very wrathy, and flourishing a rod over James' head, ordered him to translate it *again.*

but the lazy boy did not improve by either effort. Snibbens exercised James in a lively manner with the rod, around his shoulders, waist and legs.

"Listen at the·translation I give you of this simple sentence," said the teacher; and he gave James one more cut upon the ankle. "The heavens are turned around, and the night rushes from the ocean, enveloping the earth, and the sky, and the treachery of the Greeks with a great shadow." Parse *ruit*, sir."

"*Ruit* is a verb," said the whining and sobbing boy: "of the first conjugation; from *ruo, ruare, ruavi, ruatum*. Indicative mood, pluperfect tense, third person, singular number, and agrees with *Oceano*. A verb must agree with its nominative case in number and person."

"He is wrong, Mr. Snibbens," said Joe Bishop, "*ruit* is of the third conjugation."

"I am aware of that, Joe," replied the teacher. "Bring me here your dictionary. How often must I point out words to you? Do you not see as plain as the nose on your face that it comes from *ruo, ruere rui ruitum?* Now bring me here your grammar and let me show you how to find it."

Snibbens found *lego*, and whispered to himself, *lego, legis, legit, legimus, legitis, legunt*, he discovered that it was found in the indicative mood, present tense, third person, singular number, and agreed with *nox*.

"Take this lesson over again, boys, and if you come up here again so deficient I will make you remember me."

Snibbens was an industrious teacher, who, when he

was master of a subject, could impart instruction admirably. "*Primus, secundus, tertius,*" repeated the boys.
"That is right, now go to your seats and study hard.
Remember that 'labor overcomes all difficulties.'"

When Mr. Snibbens was bothered and had to refer
to his keys and translations, an excuse was easily
framed for a visit to the private room. He made good
pens, wrote a fair hand, ciphered tolerably well, was a
fluent reader, and made extensive displays with his
magic lantern. Those were the reasons that his patrons, who had not suspected his deficiency, supposed
him to be a wonderful genius.

The foundation of a boy's education is frequently
spoiled forever by just such teachers as Snibbens, who
may be found in all communities. They adopt teaching
as a profession, because it is a good stepping-stone to
the law, medicine and divinity. It is often made a sinecure by ignorant men, who succeed in humbugging a
community by artifice, and plausibility of speech.

Mr. Snibbens was as punctual to his business as the
dial is true to the sun; yet he aspired to the knowledge
of sciences and languages, of which he was entirely
ignorant. The more intelligent of the lads, who had
been placed under his literary guardianship, were certain that his instructions were not in the least beneficial
to them. They had often hinted their suspicious to
their parents, but a father who has forgotten the familiar lessons which he learned in his youth, is not a proper
judge of the qualifications of a teacher. Trustees of
academies and high schools are more frequently chosen

on account of their wealth and influence, than for their literary accomplishments. Snibbens had maintained his position unshocked and unshaken against more than one competitor more competent to fill the position than himself, at several annual meetings of the BOARD. Every one acknowledged that Snibbens was a good, clever man, and it would have been such a pity to have ejected him from his position, when the boys liked him so well: and he was such a nice, handy gentleman to instruct the Sunday School classes. No one could raise the hymns in church better than he could, and if one of the neighbors should be taken sick, he was the best hand to sit up, in the town. He was just the man who could have obtained his board in a family regardless of compensation, repaying the worthy proprietor of the house with no other coin than the pious example he might set before the children.

CHAPTER IV.

It is related of the renowned Gil Blas, that when he left the parental roof to seek his fortune in the wide, wide world, his mother bestowed upon him the last shilling she possessed, and shed copious tears at his departure; while his father enriched him with his blessing, and gently pushed him out into the arena of life. The father often means to bestow a blessing upon a son when he forces him to buffet the waves of the sea of life, though the son may place a different construction upon the actions of the father, and accuse him of cruelty. Be this as it may, if an individual is compelled to undergo hardships, and sense is to be learned only in the school of experience, youth is the proper season to receive such costly instructions; for then their admonitions will be lasting.

Mortimer Rockford had been the architect of his own magnificent fortune, and had worked his way up to the enviable position he now occupied, by persevering industry. His father died while he was a mere boy, bequeathing to his son only a moderate competency. By studied economy his mother was enabled to procure subsistence for herself and son. Through the assistance of friends and his own scanty patrimony, Mortimer was enabled to receive a Collegiate education. He graduated with distinction, and his valedictory was received with rapturous applause. His mother welcomed him back to the cottage with warm embraces and eyes streaming with the tears of affection. She had often denied herself the necessaries of life to lay by a small sum to purchase clothes for her darling boy. He saw the world before him as the great theatre upon which was to be enacted the great drama of life. With a bold and dauntless heart, he was contented to step upon the boards and perform his part. He had early learned that life is a commingling of the good and the evil, and that man, in a great measure, holds the reins of happiness in his own hands.

What a strange mortal am I, thought Mortimer, if, with the knowledge I possess of human nature, and the modicum of learning that I have gleaned from the instructions of wise men, I shall not be enabled to buffet the waves of any stream upon which my life-boat may be hereafter cast? I have only to maintain a firm position upon any question that presents itself to my mind, and combat Prejudice and Ignorance with the weapons of Reason and Common Sense, to obtain the mastery.

Mortimer had not taken into consideration that fortune or position was to be gained by other than close management. Neither of the twain is the result of any certain plan of action. Men who have been noted for chicanery. industry and economy, have as often failed of arriving at distinction, or been disappointed in the accumulation of bags of golden coins, as those who have waited for

the waves of prosperity to waft them upon a golden
beach.   He had adopted the law as his profession,
though his fees had been meager in the beginning, and
at first he was almost denied the means of subsistence;
yet Themis, at times, poured into his coffers bountiful
showers of gold.

Fifteen years of incessant labor and toil found Mortimer, surely but slowly, ascending to the topmost round of
the ladder in his profession.   He had been a friend to
the needy, had combatted and contended with error in
all its forms and phases, and Fame was almost within
his grasp.   He had nearly overcome the asperities of
life, had passed the rapids of man's existence and was
just entering upon the gulf of happiness, when the
flower of his youth was beginning to fade.   He was a
famous lawyer and bade fair to arrive at eminence within
a few years, when Miss Josephine Broxton, the belle of
the State, enriched him with her heart and hand, and
encumbered him with a magnificent dowry.

Mr. Rockford built one of the most costly edifices
that was ever erected in the environs of Crofton.   It
was in Crofton that he was born and reared, and it was
there that he wished to pass the remaining years of his
life.   Heaven had smiled upon and blessed him, and it
was far from his purpose to desert the scenes of his
childhood.   Five hundred acres of arable land were attached to his homestead, and the products of the labor
of his slaves were more than equal to his expenditures.
Mr. Rockford would have been a mere madman had he
not appreciated all those advantages of fortune.   He

was admired, courted, and almost worshipped by the good citizens of the place, yet he was not vain of the position he occupied. Honors were showered thick upon him, yet he bore them with meekness.

His lovely wife was many years his junior, yet she seemed dearer in his eyes, for the discrepancy of age, and she, as a tender vine, clung still closer to him for protection. If she sighed, it was only when he was not near; if she grieved, it was at such times as the business and cares of life were too onerous for the comfort of her husband. She had studied his nature, and his every want was known to her. She had learned to read the workings of his mind by the expression of his features, and he should not have been surprised that all of his domestic wants were anticipated. One year of domestic bliss glided by, and Sebastian blessed the nuptial couch. The house of Rockford was gay with festivities when this lovely child gladdened the hearts of his devoted parents. They were now united by a strong and heavenly tie. The father had an impetus to speed him still higher up the ladder of Fame, and the mother had a tender infant to nourish, which might rise up hereafter and call her blessed.

Two joyous years passed by, and Sebastian was the lovely child of Rockford house, as he appeared upon the eventful night of the murder of Mr. Winslow. His mother had lain him quietly in his bed and drawn the coverlids gently over him, and sat down to amuse herself by the perusal of a favorite book, until the return of her husband. She was not uneasy about Mr. Rockford until the hour of ten had arrived, and he came not. She had scarcely ever known him to remain from home longer than the appointed time for his return. She turned over the leaves of the book with an air of seriousness, as the steady stroke of the pendulum vibrated upon her ear and forced the obedient hands of the clock to move in their accustomed sphere. Eleven o'clock, and still her husband came not. She went to the casement and looked anxiously in the direction of the town. Wearied out by fruitless vigils, she took her seat by the fire and gave vent to her grief by a copious shower of tears. In a short time her husband came. The explanation he gave for remaining beyond his limited time, relieved her mind of much anxiety, yet the death of an estimable citizen was a sufficient cause of her sharing the despondency of her husband. Blessed Josephine! if no deeper sorrows ever fall to thy lot than to weep for departed friends, thou wilt not share the fortune of those whom adversity has marked out for its prey.

The next morning, while the Rockfords were seated at the breakfast-table, the conversation took a turn from a lisping word which fell from the lips of Sebastian. He had been dividing his breakfast with Jupe, until the little dog became impatient of being fed by driblets, and seized hold of one of the boy's feet with his teeth, and playfully bit it, while Sebastian dealt him a few hearty blows with his spoon, declaring in his broken style of speech, that Jupe should sleep no more in his little sailboat.

"Josephine," said Mr. Rockford, "this is a cool,

wintry, sunshiny morning. Suppose we take Sebastian and the nurse, and go upon a sailing excursion."

"Nothing will give me more pleasure than to gratify you, my husband," said the affectionate wife. "Besides, Sebastian and myself both need exercise and a change of air. The breeze has just sprung up, and as there are no indications of a storm, we will set out upon the excursion as soon as I can prepare a sufficient supply of provisions for the day."

"You need not tarry for that purpose, my love," said the husband, "the ship Ellen is anchored only a league from shore, and her commander has given me several pressing invitations to visit him before he leaves the port. When once we have ascended upon the deck of his ship, I am certain we will be close prisoners for the day."

The preparations for their departure were soon made. Seated in the pleasure-boat that was kept for the especial accommodation of the family, the Rockfords were soon sailing upon the bosom of the Atlantic. Sebastian would clap his hands for joy when a porpoise would emerge from the waves in its rotary evolutions. The sea gulls would almost strike the sails of the boat with their snowy wings, as if they were tendering to the party a joyous welcome to the crested waves.

"Look, Josephine, how small the sails and hull of the ship appear in the distance. The wings of that gull that flew by then, are large in comparison to the rigging of the ship, at this distance. Within the space of an hour, if no accidents befall us, we will be upon the deck of

3

that ship which is larger than the castle we have left
behind us."

"True, Mr. Rockford, the pleasures of life, like the
uncertain future, are in the distance, yet we are not
sure of ever having them within our grasp. A slight
misguidance of the pilot at the helm, a sudden and un-
looked for storm springing up, and the possibility of
our reaching the ship would be only in the scope of
Omnipotence."

"But, Josephine, suppose we should have no faith in
the security of our boat, and entirely distrust the capacity of the pilot, would we not despair of reaching the
point of our destination? Why have we deserted the
land and embarked upon the sea? You answer, for a
change, and to gratify a mere whim. We live to learn,
and desire to see what we have learned to admire, from
descriptions of good authors. As young as Sebastian
is, the scenes of this day may never fade from his mind.
His memory as yet is as a dream, but striking scenes
may awake it to a reality. One hour to a child is as
long as a day to an adult. Frequent changes of scenery
are beneficial to them, yet it is better for them to go but
little into the company of strangers."

The breeze blew briskly, and the helmsman performed
his part well. The boat was soon snugly secured along-
side of the ship. In a few minutes the party ascended
the ship's ladder, and were ushered into the spacious
saloon. The rocking of the vessel was at first unpleas-
ant to Josephine, whose voyages had been confined principally to the inland boat travel and pleasure excursions

along the beach. Sebastian was perfectly amazed to
see so many objects of attraction. The door knobs,
locks, tippings and castors upon the chairs, occupied his
attention. He rolled the single ottomans about, to the
amusement of the Captain, who took quite a fancy to
him, and had him supplied with candies and nuts in
abundance. Captain Walsingham was an old friend
and college-mate of Mr. Rockford's, and had frequently
spent a day with him at Rockford house, while the
Ellen was lying in port.

"My dear Mrs. Rockford," said the polite Captain,
"it affords me much pleasure to welcome you and my
friend of former days aboard of my vessel. It is a
pleasure I have long sought and heartily desired. The
best plan that we can conceive of, by which to preserve
old friendships, is cordial and happy re-unions."

"You are extremely kind, Captain Walsingham.—
The friends of my husband merit my respect."

Mrs. Rockford was left to amuse herself with Sebastian an hour or two, while the gentlemen went upon
deck to enjoy a fine cigar. The ship maids, who attended to the ladies' saloon, were directed to pay her
especial attention and spread the table with luncheon.
Rockford and Captain Walsingham, each, provided with
a spy-glass, amused themselves a few minutes in taking
observations, but discovered only a few fishing smacks
and oyster boats.

"See those restless, toiling men; how they spread
and draw in their nets? How they laugh and shout
when a large quantity of fish is bagged? The oyster

catchers are playing havoc with the mollusk tribe. One of the crew has just raised the grapplers from the deep bed, and another is receiving the huge mass. Large quantities are produced from one mother shell, around which they cling until their own weight breaks them off into sections."

"Look again," said Rockford in reply to the Captain; "one of the men has fallen overboard. The waves have almost washed him from their reach. Now they have succeeded in throwing him a line. He is safe among them again, and they are applying a canteen of spirits to his lips. What a happy set of fellows they must be?"

"Yes, indeed," replied the Captain, "they think but little of the past, and the future to them is not penetrated by hopes or fears. They are 'hale fellows well met,' who make the most of the present time. I have frequent visits from men of this class while lying at anchor in various ports. They barter large quantities of fish and oysters to me for provisions. Those men you see at the bar paid me a visit yesterday, and I purchased some of their cargo."

"I think," said Rockford, "they are the sea-faring portion of the fish-mongers who dwell in those filthy huts near our wharf."

"It is highly probable," replied the Captain. "They related to me yesterday, that they had been attacked by a party of desperate looking men in boats, and their fish and oysters taken from them. They supposed that the men were a portion of banditti, who have a retreat not many miles from shore."

"This must be looked into," rejoined Rockford. "The police must have the country diligently searched."

The gentlemen, arm in arm, walked the quarter-deck, talking socially about their college scrapes. Their merry peals of laughter often attracted the attention of the crew, who were busily engaged in hoisting packages of merchandise from the hold of the vessel and lowering them upon the lighter, or scow, which was to convey them across the bar to Crofton. The friends continued their walk, and the jolly crew sang their songs and turned the windlass. They were devoted to the Captain, and his slightest command was executed by every one, from the mate down to the sailor-boy.

When the dinner hour appproached, Captain Walsingham led the way to the saloon, where Mrs. Rockford and Sebastian were. The little boy had made friends with a large Newfoundland dog belonging to Captain Walsingham.

"Sebastian is very fond of dogs," said his father. "He has a little pet at home which is as dear to him as his parents."

"He shall have the Newfoundland, too, if you will be encumbered with him, Rockford," remarked the Captain. "Carlo is a royal dog, and will guard any treasure with fidelity that may be placed under his care."

"I accept the gift for Sebastian with much pleasure." said Rockford.

Dinner was announced, and the party were soon seated at a table which was spread with all the delicacies of the season. When the first and second courses were ended, the wines and fruits were brought out.

Those who have never partaken of a meal on ship-
board are not prepared to appreciate good eating. The
meal was finished, and the evening was spent in witness-
ing the feats of strength, agility, and the dances of the
sailors. The Rockfords were perfectly delighted with
their excursion; and it was with regret they took leave
of the Captain, who accompanied them in his boat more
than half the distance to the town. Carlo only parted
with his master by compulsion. He was tied to one of
the rings of the boat, and struggled and howled piteously when his master put back to the ship.

Just as the sun dipped his red disc into the sea, the
Rockfords stepped on shore and sought their home. The
servants made fast the boat, and took home the oars and
the disconsolate Carlo, who, if he had been let loose at
that moment, would have swum to his master's ship
again.

CHAPTER V.

It is a difficult thing, indeed, to give racy descriptions of the scenes of every-day life ; but those descriptions if faithfully portrayed, are more eagerly read, and produce a more lasting impression on the mind than a treatise upon abstruse subjects. Divest literature of its common-place scenes, which are introduced by authors to fill up the acts of the drama, and you remove one of the main props which support the fabric of fiction. One writer may spin out numberless pages upon an evening excursion, and sustain a fair reputation for authorship, yet the trivial scenes, clothed in such beautiful language, will scarcely survive the first edition of a work. The imagination of the reader may not be so lucid as that of the writer, and it becomes necessary to paint each scene with appropriate colors. Another writer may introduce characters of an heroic caste into his work, yet if the picture is not faithfully sketched, and the back-ground made to correspond with the subject-matter, the delineator has mixed his colors in vain.

Some of the most noted authors have preferred to introduce the best scenes of their works in the opening chapters, in order that the attention of the reader may at once be arrested, but the denouement of the plot may expand into airy nothingness. The Illiad of Homer, one of the most beautiful poems that was ever written in any language, and perfect in all its parts, is a remarkable exception to the general rule, inasmuch as the illustrious author plunges into *medias res*, and presents the hero in a revengeful mood, about to decide the destinies of two great, contending nations, by retiring from the war which his valor alone could win. But is it not preferable to commence with the beginning, and enjoy the pleasure of filling up each scene in the life of your hero; not leaving it for the imagination of the reader to supply the vacuum? The taste of the intelligent reader is the best arbiter.

Such a thing has happened, where self-styled critics have disputed about the identity of the rightful hero or heroine of a novel. It is an evidence of an erratic genius to clothe the hero in habiliments so similar to those of the prominent characters, that the distinction is difficult. For fear that some critics may wrangle about the hero of this work, it is proper to state right here that Sebastian, and not his father, is the hero of this novel. Who would care to record the actions of a more promising lad than the little curly haired boy that was the light and life of Rockford house?

A few days subsequent to the advent of the Newfoundland dog to his new home, Sebastian was playing in the veranda with his pets. Carlo was one of the largest size of his species, while Jupe was the most diminutive of his race. The one was large, muscular and well adapted to the performance of feats that required both strength and agility; the other was exceedingly small, feeble, and seemed to have been formed for a plaything and pest. Carlo was as much astonished at the little creature, as Jupe was at the huge proportions of his powerful companion. Jupe had all the mettle of a bull-dog concentrated in his heart. At times, when Carlo would irritate him, he would bite him upon the nose with all the vengeance of an adder. The only punishment Carlo inflicted upon him for his misdeeds was both laughable and tantalizing. He would seize Jupe carefully around the body and bear him off between his huge jaws. After running across the yard a few times, at a pace so brisk that the poodle would lose his breath, Carlo would deposit the culprit upon the steps of the veranda for resuscitation.

Sebastian had learned to ride upon the back of Carlo with perfect safety. Upon the morning on which the boy and his pets were introduced upon the veranda, Sebastian had just finished feeding them. His mother, hearing her son express a desire to ride, walked out upon the veranda and placed him upon Carlo's back. Jupe expressed a desire to ride also, by holding up his fore-paws and barking piteously. Mrs. Rockford placed Jupe in Sebastian's arms. Carlo had not the least objection in the world to carrying his young master, but with the addition of Jupe to his burden he trotted off that morning in no good frame of mind. If the weight of Jupe had not been the hundredth fraction of an ounce, the principle would have been the same with the crest-fallen Carlo. He laid up a good shaking for the poodle when the next overt act should be committed.

Carlo carried his riders out upon the lawn in front of

the spacious mansion, where he met Mr. Rockford just
returning from town.   The parent was much delighted
at the sport of Sebastian and Jupe.   He conducted the
obedient Carlo back to the house, where he was disen-
cumbered of his load.

Mr. Rockford was particularly fond of the enjoyments
of home.   His early years had been spent upon the
arena of a busy life; and when the period had arrived
for him to assume the responsibilities of a married man,
the major portion of his leisure hours was passed in
the bosom of his family.

When Mr. Rockford seated Sebastian by his side in
the sitting room on that morning, the curiosity of the
boy was greatly exercised about the contents of his
father's pockets.   As was his usual custom, he diligently searched them until he was enabled to draw forth his
candies and fruits, which were usually stored in those
receptacles in large quantities.

"What news do you bring from town, Mr. Rockford?"
said the wife, as she seated herself for the purpose of
resuming her never-ending work of embroidery.

"There are strange rumors afloat in Crofton," replied
Mr. Rockford.   "They say there is a band of robbers
not many miles from the town.   Several suspicious men
have been seen lurking about the jail since the confinement of Royston, and it is now believed that he has
been mysteriously connected with them for two or three
years.   His frequent visits to the country upon horse-
back, during that space of time, and returning late at
night, are strong presumptive evidence that he knows

more about those lawless men than he cares to relate. The jailor has been instructed by the proper authorities to have the prisoner closely guarded."

Mr. Rockford had a select library. Every good work of ancient and modern times formed his tasty collection. Shakspeare, Milton, Pope and Dryden were his favorite poets. It was from them he had derived that exquisite taste in the selection of words that lent so much beauty to his speeches. He had perused a thousand books before he was thoroughly convinced that all knowledge is contained in a few volumes. He was fond of reading histories, particularly those that contained the records of ancient heroes. He had learned to divide the reigns of princes of different kingdoms into periods. He was never at a loss how to place events in their proper chronological order. His law books were never neglected, being read and studied by him with system. The English and American Reports of the decisions of cases at Common Law, were as familiar to him as household words. It was a thorough knowledge of those works, and a practical application of the same, that rendered him so formidable a competitor to his compeers at the bar.

He employed his time chiefly in the investigation of his cases, when not too busily engaged in the mechanical formulas of the profession. He was never taken by surprise when one of his cases was called in Court. The Spring Session of the Superior Court was to commence within a few weeks, and he bent all his energies upon a proper preparation for the prosecution of Roys-

ton, as Mr. Winslow had retained him as leading counsel.   He was a conscientious man, who did not desire
to receive five thousand dollars without rendering his
client an equivalent for the same.

Time ever speeds by rapidly when we are engaged.
An unusually large gathering about the Court House
square gave indications that the Court was upon the
point of convening.

The Spring had come in that warm, beautiful clime of
the South, and Nature had put on a gay dress.   The
woods were enameled with flowers, and every hedge
was green with vernal beauty.   The feathered songsters
sang their matins from the bush, and every animated
creature rejoiced in the return of Spring.   Beautiful,
happy season, would that thy reign could last forever!

The Grand Jury found a true bill against Royston
for murder, during the first day of the Session, and
when the case was called up, an unusually large crowd
assembled to witness the trial.   The counsel for Royston did their duty to their client, but so well was the
case managed upon the part of the prosecution, a motion for a new trial was not made, though many were
the points they strove to make during the examination of the witnesses.   Royston was convicted, and
sentence of death was pronounced upon him.

Mr. Rockford had made one of his ablest efforts upon
the trial of Royston, and through his adroit management of the case, the Jury were enabled to bring in a
verdict against him, although there was some rebutting
evidence in his favor.   His speech upon the occasion

was one of the crowning acts of his life. He had never been known to make a failure at the bar, but, upon this occasion, his success was commensurate with the fame he had previously achieved as a criminal lawyer. The Court House was filled to overflowing with the citizens. and strangers from the neighboring counties, who had been induced to attend, to listen to the speech of a distinguished man in a case of such vital importance to the State and community. Mr. Rockford received the congratulations of his friends with that degree of modesty natural to one so gifted.

Duty, in his eyes, was more to be valued than the hue and cry after popularity. Unless he considered that he was entitled to commendation, he would have shrunk from applause, and desired his friends to have lavished their praises upon one more deserving. Popularity is like the current of a stream, the more auxiliaries it receives, the more swollen will be the current. and the more readily will it be enabled to overcome obstacles in its headlong course. But, instead of endeavoring to augment his popularity, Rockford discouraged all propositions tending to his own advancement.

The law, especially the criminal portion. is fraught with many difficulties. It is not an easy task to reconcile the law with the evidence and make a point : nor is it less difficult to convince a client that justice has been done to him, or a culprit that no advantage has been taken of his dependent condition. Those who embark in the profession must make up their minds to sail upon a tempestuous sea. It is very much to be feared that

the majority of lawyers become case-hardened, after a
few years of successful practice; but it must be remembered that all secular professions have their abuses.

Mr. Rockford had never courted the popular favor of
the world for his advancement to honorable positions,
but his mind had been bent almost entirely upon the
acquisition of PROPERTY. He had seen the advantages
arising from the influence of WEALTH. If he did not
acknowledge its power, the WORLD did. It is as profit-
able to blow your breath against the whirlwind as to
move in opposition to the popular current. The actions
of one man may be Herculean in comparison to those of
another; yet, when weighed in the balance against the
deeds of thousands, the scales are turned upon the side
of the majority. Some contend that the whole force of
government is ruled by compromises, but its own ab-
surdity refutes the admission. A party which admits
the force of compromises, will have but little else to do
but to make and support them. Rockford was a happy
exception to men who are guided, in the main, by con-
ventional rules. He steered very safely between Scylla
and Charybdis, neither asking nor courting popular
favor.

Thirty years ago, the period at which this story
opens, our Government was supported more according
to the tenets of JUSTICE, TRUTH and MODERATION, than
it has been of late years. There was not such an in-
equality in the dispensation of justice, as at the present
time. The contending parties, if they differed materially, based the discrepancy of their views upon other

than sectional grounds. If the laws, then, were rightly administered, and made to redound to the glory and happiness of a State, the cause was attributed to the correctness of self-government. If a State is *made* to bear the burdens of other sections of a Federal Government, the remedy to correct the evil is not within its own hands, and there is no virtue, then, in State Sovereignty while the people submit.

Rockford was not a mercenary man, but he had a sufficient quantity of pride to speed him forward in the performance of anything in which he thought his DUTY was enlisted. He had made a powerful effort to convict Royston of the heinous crime of murder, and had succeeded. He did not fear or care for the consequences while his conscience was not disquieted. It had been intimated to him that Royston was not without friends, and the promptness with which competent counsel had been employed to defend him, corroborated this belief. It was supposed that he had been intimately connected with a band of robbers, whose depradations, of late, were assuming an importance not to be overlooked by those who had rights to maintain. It was even supposed that the wire-workers of that band were frequent visitors to the town, and might he not have endangered his life and property by discharging his duty so well? Admitting this to be true, he had pledged himself to be faithful to his trust, and no obstructions could thwart his plans, or remove him from the course of his duty.

The laws had been seriously violated, the life of a good citizen had been unjustly taken, and was it a proper time to compromise the rights of humanity to escape the prejudices of those who were not law-abiding? He belonged to that class of men who were in favor of letting justice be done, though the heavens should fall Do you not applaud him?

CHAPTER VI.

SWEET, holy, heavenly Sabbath, who does not love to behold thy coming? Who does not admit thy right to be classed among things divine? It is the type of that endless rest which God hath prepared in the Heavens for His people. In whatever country of this beautiful world, upon which the Gospel of Christ has poured its blessings, the Sabbath is respected and observed. God is truly in His Holy temple, and earth should keep silent before Him. The citizens of Crofton were moral, and the crowded pews of the churches attested the interest they took in religion. There were but few, indeed, whom an idle curiosity ever led to the sanctuary. It was a pleasing sight, upon each Sabbath morning, to behold the avenues and streets leading to the churches, crowded with people hurrying on to worship at the shrine of God.

The carriages of the wealthy drew up at the churchyard, and the occupants passed quietly into the house of the Most High. The middle classes and the poor all thronged the aisles of the church, and crowded into the unrented pews. Each one remembered the beautiful sentence, "I was glad when they said unto me, Let us go unto the house of the Lord."

The church of Christ will never be advanced in in-

4

terest where the fashions and prejudices of the citizens are allowed to govern it. If wealth were more equally distributed among the people, a moderate degree of splendor might not be objectionable. But the majority of those who are constant attendants upon Divine service belong to the class of those who are supported by their daily labor. They never feel at home in the midst of so much splendor as is sometimes lavished upon the decorations of churches. Whatever may be the views of others upon this subject, we respect them; but if money is to be spent in a good cause, let it be given to the poor, for we have them with us always.

The organ struck up an anthem, and the choir joined in sweet harmony. The Minister read out the morning lesson, and his fervent prayers ascended to Heaven. In his discourse he alluded feelingly to the recent painful occurrence. Tears of sorrow were shed by those who beheld the grief of the father and mother of Mr. Winslow, who occupied one of the front seats. The Minister bade them weep not for their son, but to prepare to meet the great day of the coming of God. It was a difficult thing for them to submit to the will of Providence, but God hath commanded us to let the dead bury their dead. and we should repine not. The Savior of mankind suffered death for us, and lay in the cold embraces of the tomb, and we should not dread to enter there.

He dwelt upon the enormity of the sins of those who rejected the Gospel, and did not heed the warnings that were given them every day. The whole congregation felt the force of the appeal, and when the benediction was pronounced, and the congregation departed for their homes, each one felt that he or she had received a blessing.

Mr. Rockford and his family were conveyed to their splendid mansion in their costly carriage. When they were summoned to dinner, the husband and wife commenced the meal in silence, but they were soon engaged in social converse.

"My dear," said Mr. Rockford, "is it not strange that we who enjoy so many blessings, should live so neglectful in the performance of our duty?"

A tear glistened in the eye of Mrs. Rockford, as she heard this confession from the lips of her husband. She knew that he was not what the world calls a wicked man, but his mind had been so bent upon the acquisition of property that he had been too negligent in returning thanks to God for the many blessings with which he was surrounded."

"Truly, my husband, we are all too sinful. We are too apt to forget God while He is so good to us. It is only when his afflicting rod is scourging us that we remember Him. He afflicts us that we may be drawn more closely into His fold. Suppose He should take Sebastian from us, would we not be bowed down with sorrow?"

As the eyes of Mr. Rockford rested upon the beautiful face of his child, his heart was filled with pride mingled with sorrow. He knew that if the boy should be spared to him, his own life might flow on in one uninterrupted stream of happiness, but should an early death remove him from the home of his dear parents, that sorrow would fill that house forevermore.

Mr. Rockford had arrived at the period of life when it behooved him to render those around him all the assistance that lay in his power. He resolved from that day to commence a reform. His example might tend much towards influencing others to leave off from following in the evil paths of sin.

But how to commence that reform was certainly a difficult thing. As he sat in his studio upon that holy Sabbath evening, and beheld with what glee Sebastian sported among the flowers that were just opening to the kisses of Spring, he felt as if his Maker had sent his son as a blessing, and his own example would either prepare his offspring for happiness, or consign him to the shades of misery.

He had endeavored to live justly and conform to the laws of the land, but, upon an examination of his own heart, he discovered that the laws of God required more than the mere observance of a creed which is upheld merely by the basis of morality. He had been influenced too much by the subtle teachings of those who, though not militating against the established usages of orthodox church doctrines, invited them to pin their faith to moral principles, which were not dissimilar to those tenets taught by the ancient philosophers.

He had not sought his knowledge, in a prayerful manner, from the great fountain of divinity — the Bible. Henceforth he would not neglect the blessed volume. If any of our readers are in doubt as to any question which should guide them aright, in a moral point of view, let them search the Scriptures — the tenets of men are dangerous guides.

The Sabbath passed, and the week with its busy scenes was ushered in. Each one of the citizens of the place was busy in the pursuit of his daily occupation. Mr. Snibbens had turned over several new leaves in his classics, and as many in his translations. His scholars were flogged and "turned back" when they advanced too rapidly for him. Mr. Samuel Culverhouse and his amiable wife still prepared wholesome viands for their boarders. Mr. Simpkins sold his goods to those who gave him their patronage, and the affairs of the town moved on smoothly. The Ellen had been heavily laden with the staple produce of the country, and had sailed to foreign ports. The Captain promised Mr. Rockford to pay him a visit upon his return, and bring many curiosities and presents for Sebastian, for whom he had manifested much love.

Those who dwell in fine houses, and are blest with the goods of this world, are rarely, if ever, wanting in friends and relatives. Rockford house was noted for its hospitality. A few days after the Sabbath evening reveries of the proprietor, several friends alighted at his gate. Mr. Rockford felt that it was not good to be alone, and he hastened to welcome them. As he hastened across the long front yard, which intervened between the house and the outer street, he recognized several friends and relatives whom he had not seen for several years. He should now have an opportunity of presenting them to his dear Josephine. She had never seen them, but his friends were ever dear to her.

"My dear aunt Margery," said Mr. Rockford, "how

glad I am to see you! Welcome to Rockford house.
Cousin Roxana, this is indeed a surprise. Josephine
will be so glad to see you. Cousin Frances, how you
have grown! Mr. Watson, you and Mr. Judson assist
the ladies to the house, while I look after your bag-
gage."

Mrs. Rockford, arriving just at this time, was for-
mally presented to each one of her guests by her husband. They were conducted to the spacious mansion
by the good lady. Rooms were speedily prepared for
the new comers, and Rockford house was no longer a
quiet residence, but it seemed more like a crowded hotel at a watering place than the dwelling of a private
family.

The horses of the visitors were properly cared for,
and soon occupied the well filled stables. The carriages
were rubbed off and rolled under the spacious sheds,
and every thing was in a happy bustle that lived, breath-
ed and moved upon that homestead. We live only for
our friends, thought Mr. Rockford, as he arrayed himself in a new suit of clothes which he had never yet
worn. Selfishness was no part of his nature, and what
he enjoyed, his friends were welcome to share with him.
He surveyed himself in the long mirror, and was not at
all displeased with his own personal appearance. It is
true a few gray hairs were intermingled with his flowing
locks, but he knew he had arrived at that period of life
when gray hairs were expected. We have said he was
satisfied with his appearance. The reader would have
acknowledged Mr. Rockford's claims to fine looks, we

will not say to beauty, for that term should never be applied to men.

As we have said before, Rockford house was the very home of hospitality. The building was very large, and commanded, not only a good view of the ocean, but a person stationed in the observatory might overlook the whole region. The eight spacious rooms upon the first floor were occupied, principally, by the family and the select friends and relatives who blessed the house with their protracted visits. The eight rooms on the second floor were used as the apartments of those who were merely *spending* a few days as *friends*. The four rooms of the third story were occupied when the house was crowded to overflowing. Those rooms were resorted to by Mr. Rockford, when he wished to retire from the din and bustle of his family. The front of the building was adorned with massive columns, which extended from the main piazza to the roofing, giving beauty and strength to the entire structure. At the landing of the second and third stories, a veranda extended out for the accommodation of a small party who might desire to enjoy a tete-a-tete, and yet have the benefit of the sea breezes. The house was built of brick, and stuccoed after the most approved style, and so accurately penciled as to present the appearance of a grand marble pile. Every room of this magnificent structure was supplied with furniture to correspond with its external appearance. The well trained servants moved like clock-work in their appointed spheres. Few were the orders given at Rockford house, for when the ser-

vants, who know their duty, perform it. system is never
wanting.

Mrs. Margery Fairfield was an aunt of Mr. Rockford's.   She was a lady of moderate fortune, who resided at Colonna, one of the neighboring towns.   Her
husband had died only a few years previous to the visit
of the good lady to her relative.   Her two daughters.
Roxana and Frances, who had completed their education, were her only children.   Thomas Watson and
Reginald Judson were agreeable acquaintances, who
had kindly consented to be their visiting companions.

After the visitors had been conducted to their rooms,
and sufficient time had elapsed for them to perform their
ablutions, and exchange a traveling for a more comely
dress, the company assembled in the drawing-room.   It
was a goodly sight to see how the countenance of each
one was wreathed with smiles.   Mr. Rockford could but
anticipate a pleasant time with his visitors.   If time
should pass sluggishly, and the hours should be inter-
spersed with moments of gloom, his carriages or pleasure-boat should be put into requisition.

Mr. Rockford again welcomed the party to his house.
and wished them to put off all restraint and seek what
means of enjoyment that might be within their grasp.
The company were soon engaged in an animated conversation, in which Mr. Rockford and aunt Margery
took the lead.   The young men, the cousins and Mrs.
Rockford were not long in becoming acquainted.   Sebastian and his pets were not overlooked.   At length.
when the party had expressed a desire to promenade

upon the terraces, Mr. Rockford led them out in front of the building. They were struck with admiration at the beauty of the evergreen hedges, and the vast quantity of early Spring flowers, which were thus early scenting the lawn. The area just in front of the house bloomed with flowers. A little farther on, the giant oaks, and the trees which were planted by the proprietor of the place, covered the ground with a continuous shade.

After spending an hour in an agreeable conversation, and enjoying a delightful walk, the company retired to their rooms to make preparations for dinner.

What mortal is there, who is free from the horrible pangs of dyspepsia, that does not welcome the dinner hour? Poems have been written upon it, orations have been pronounced upon it, yet the theme is inexhaustible. The ancients revered it; the moderns do not scorn it; and we, oh! Epicurus, do not hate it. Take away our breakfast or supper, but let us not be far distant from the smoking viands that roast upon the spit, or the brown pheasants that float in the golden gravy, with all the little extras that fill up the spare corners of the ovens. Let us not be far from those when the tintinnabulation of the dinner-bell is heard.

Reader, did you ever enjoy a good dinner when twenty miles of travel had given you a good appetite, and you had become sick of home fare? If not, you have yet something to live for.

CHAPTER VII.

The majority of mankind rejoice in the blessings that
are poured out upon them from day to day, without returning thanks to the great Giver of good and perfect
gifts.   It is a common saying, that 'the hog never looks
up to him who threshes down the acorns.'   It is never
more perfectly exemplified than in the conduct of some
men, who seem to be perfectly devoid of all moral principle.

Fortune, it is true, showers its blessings, indiscrim-
inately, upon the just and unjust.   The rains of Heaven
descend with equal measure upon saint and sinner; the
fortunes of the hour are within the grasp of the prince
and the peasant.   Whether the happiness of our little
hero is controlled entirely by chance, or not, the writer
deposeth not.

We, at present, must follow the happy party into the
spacious hall of Rockford house.   It was arranged with
every convenience that modern taste could fashion out.
We shall not give a minute description of it, leaving the
imagination of the reader to ornament the scenes.

The table was bountifully spread with costly viands,
which could not fail to tempt the palate of the most
fastidious.   Mr. Rockford seated himself at the head
of the well-supplied board, and bade his guests be seat-

ed and enjoy the bounties of Rockford house. It was his peculiar delight to have his friends surround his table, and enjoy the comforts of his well filled larder. Conversation is the fountain from which flows the source of enjoyment at the dinner-table. Without its aid, the sumptuous feast is spread in vain. The most marked attention upon the part of the host, without a due appreciation of the guests, is a vain effort to effect enjoyment. Mr. Rockford had studied the philosophy of the ancients and the more refined of the moderns, and was prepared, upon all occasions, to render any company into which he mignt be thrown, agreeable.

"Homer had a pleasant and very agreeable faculty. Mr. Watson," said Mr. Rockford, "of describing a feast, and lending to the assembly a grandiloquent flow of conversation, to enliven it."

"True," replied the guest, who was never more at home than in descanting upon his favorite authors. "Homer supposed, and that truthfully, that a feast without conversation was a ludicrous thing. It would have appeared in his eyes, as if the guests had been invited to a funeral, rather than to the board of merriment, if the flow of sentiment were of consequence obliged to be restricted."

"Who has not been touched with the lines in Homer?

"Then spread the tables, the repast prepare,
Each takes his seat, and each receives his share.
When now the rage of hunger was repressed,
With pure libations they conclude the feast."

"But," replied Mr. Watson, "the sentiment, as expressed in those lines, is rather an invitation to youth to enjoy the luxuries of the wine cup."

"Not at all," said the good host. "In those days, when liquors were unadulterated, there was but little drunkenness. Men were supposed to be guided more by reason and common sense than they are now. The feast, or even an extraordinary dining, was not supposed to be complete without the introduction of wine. If men would only drink the juice of the grape in moderation, we should have no cases of intoxication."

Mr. Judson, who had been endeavoring to entertain the ladies in the meantime, joined in the conversation, and the meal passed off to the satisfaction of every one present. The meats, dainties, fruits and wines were served in turn. When the last course was served, the company retired from the hall to enjoy the evening as the fates might decree, or as their host might see proper.

He is a happy man who can make the best plans for enjoyment. The wisest men have failed in this particular. In vain we often sit and ponder over the best matured plans of action. The occurrences of an hour may supply us with the means of enjoyment, or may snatch from us every vestige of that basis of enjoyment which may be fraught with pleasure.

The visitors of Mr. Rockford, in a very few days, became domesticated, and distant formalities were abandoned. The amusements consisted of excursions along the coast in the pleasure-boats belonging to Mr. Rockford, or the carriages conveyed the guests to the romantic portions of the surrounding country. Mr. Watson was particularly fond of the society of Miss Roxana Fairfield, the elder of the beautiful sisters, while she was not indifferent to his polite attentions. He had commenced the practice of the Law at Colonna, under the most favorable auspices. He had been received as an agreeable visitor at the house of Mrs. Fairfield; thus his acquaintance with the family had almost ripened into intimacy. He was one of those prudent young men whose good sense never permitted him to enter into extravagances of speech. He had been a close student, and had not only read the works of the best authors, but had studied them carefully. Upon this account, he was a very pleasant companion for Mr. Rockford. They spent several hours of each day in conversation upon polite literature. They were particularly fond of poetry, especially the works of the authors of the old school. It was a pleasant task for them to take the works of Pope, and select portions from his best essays and translations. Each line was suggestive of thought, and lengthy disputations would spring up between the friends, which could only be settled by an agreement upon the next beautiful passage.

Mr. Judson was a young man of a gay temperament. He seemed to live only for the enjoyment of the present. He amused Miss Frances Fairfield and Mrs. Rockford by a rehearsal of his college scrapes. To have heard him converse, one would have supposed that the four years he spent at the University were not well improved, but he had managed to pick up a smattering of the languages. He had merely *scraped* through a graduation. He was the life of the party, and never let time hang heavy if he could procure an audience.

If he could amuse himself in no other way, he would
take Jupe and Carlo and amuse Sebastian. The child
loved him dearly, and insisted upon a frequent rehearsal of the feats he had taught the pets to perform. He
would clap his little hands and jump for joy when Carlo would leap over the bars, or find a handkerchief,
hidden by Mr. Judson.

The guests had been at Rockford house several days,
and yet their host would not consent for them to depart.
Time had not passed so pleasantly with him in a long
time. He exacted a promise from them that they would
spend two more weeks at his house. He desired to give
them a grand party, and invite the citizens of the town
to it. He was fond of merriment himself, and nothing
delighted him so much as to see his friends enjoy his
hospitalities.

Aunt Margery spent the most of her time in the society of Mrs. Rockford, whose company she esteemed
very greatly. The good old lady was fond of imparting
what lessons she had early learned upon house-keeping,
the art of cookery, and the all-important one of quilt-
making, to all young folks. She had seen the folly of
throwing away scraps which might just as well form the
squares of a quilt. It would be well for us if we had
many such good souls as she was. She was not stupid
or awkward in company, but preferred the society of a
few to mingling with the gay throngs, whose only object
appeared to her to be a grand display of fine dress.
She thought folks had better learn to copy Nature more,
and trust less to art. But aunt Margery was too pru-

duent to restrict her daughters in their harmless enjoyments.

What a happy thing it was for Mrs. Rockford that she had the assistance of aunt Margery! When her husband proposed the party, she interposed not the least objection, but readily gave her consent. Her larders were well supplied with every ingredient she desired. Her cooks were well trained, and she was no novice in the culinary art. Aunt Margery could give her much good counsel; and upon the following day she commenced making extensive preparations for the festival. Her husband had told her to spare no expense, but to fit up a sumptuous supper for a great number of guests.

It was soon known in Crofton that a grand party was to be given by Mr. Rockford in honor of Mrs. Fairfield and her daughters. They had received the attentions of the visiting portion of the ladies and the young men. Those who expected tickets to the party commenced making preparations to attend. Mr. Snibbens brushed up his seedy coat, had it pressed and repaired, and commenced looking out some big words and phrases to use upon the occasion.

While the party is the common gossip of the town, and the ladies of Rockford house are making extensive preparations for the occason, let us relate other things which may be of interest to the reader. It has been intimated that a band of robbers was supposed to have one of their retreats near the town of Crofton. The attack which had been made upon the fishermen by men who seemed to be intimate with the coast, and the fact that suspicious men had been seen lurking in the neighborhood of the jail, gave strength to the suspicions that Royston had friends and accomplices in a set of marauders, who place all law and order at defiance. It was not at all improbable; neither had the character of that desperate man been above reproach for a long time. It was a mystery to his former friends and companions how he managed to pay his bills. They supposed that he had resorted to the gaming-table. His most intimate acquaintances were not generally known in the town, nor did they appear as if desirous of pushing themselves into society, so little were they suited for the company of the refined.

Crofton was built, as to the business portion of it, around the Court square. The stores of all descriptions were situated at intervals, and, with the hotels and and other buildings, filled up the entire space. The churches and academies were located upon eminences in convenient parts of the town, while the residences of the inhabitants were ranged upon the different streets, as suited the convenience of the citizen. The principal street led to the wharf, where were located the extensive ware-houses. Crofton, though not large enough to be called a city, was a place that contained nearly two thousand inhabitants; though it was a small place in comparison to some cities upon the coast.

Jewellers, druggists, dentists and painters occupied the rooms of the second and third stories of the business houses. It is to one of those out-of-the-way offices that we are about to conduct the reader. Upon a swinging sign might be read the name of "Hans Kemple, Jeweller." In order to discover the exact locality of the veritable Hans, the sign further described the part of the house he was supposed to occupy, "*Third floor, second room to the right.*" When you arrived at the gallery of the second floor, numerous signs greeted you. "Miss Jerusha Smith, Milliner." "J. Sinclair Peebles, Attorney at Law." "G. Higginbotham Compton, Dentist." "Crofton Courier," and other offices. After passing up the second flight of steps, the attention of the stranger was only directed to the small sign of Hans. The other apartments were private, or not occupied at all.

At a given signal from without, Hans went cautiously to the door, and having satisfied himself that a friend sought admittance, he opened the door without hesitation.

"Ah! Heinrich, is it you?" said Hans. "I am overjoyed to see you. How is our scheme progressing? When were you at the retreat?"

"Do not talk so loudly," replied Heinrich. "Walls have ears. You are not aware how very closely we are watched of late."

"Then come into my little back room," said Hans. "We can talk there without fear of molestation."

Hans led Heinrich through his tolerably well filled room into the small apartment indicated. The door was bolted, and they commenced talking earnestly.

"Heinrich," said Hans, "time is very precious, indeed. Only one week intervenes between this day and

5

his execution. It will never do in the world for so noble a soul as he is to suffer so humiliating a death. He has been true and valiant, and right nobly has he divided the spoils with us. He has been foremost in every attack, the first to strike, and the last to quit the field. When we have been forced to abandon an enterprise, he has covered our retreat, and defied all the united force of his assailants."

"You speak truly, Hans," said his companion. "Thus far he has borne his confinement and trial with heroic fortitude; but death is a dreadful thing. Do you suppose he would ascend the scaffold, and take the awful leap into eternity, with all the crimes that hang upon his soul, and not make a confession? You arrive at different conclusions from what I do, if you think yourself safe. He knows that it is in our power to release him from confinement, and he expects it at our hands."

"See what I have been doing for the past few days," said Hans. "Here is a finely tempered saw, which I have made. This must be conveyed to him as soon as possible. With this he can sever the manacles that bind him, and cut his way out of confinement in a few hours."

The companion of Hans informed him that he had been upon a visit to their friends, and they were doubly enlisted in the cause of Carl Royston. If he should not be enabled to make his escape within a few days, it was their intention to brave all, and risk their lives in his defence. Hans had hit upon a plan to see Royston, and he doubted not but that he could place the instrument he had made in his own hands. The jailor had called upon him only a few days before to have an article of jewelry repaired, and he would walk out in that direction and drop in and see him.

When Heinrich had taken his departure, Hans enclosed the saw, which was very small, in a paper, took several late newspapers and put them in his pocket. He directed his footsteps towards the common, upon which the jail was located. He was in the act of passing the prison, when the jailor, who was at work in the garden, hailed him, and invited him to call in. Hans tried to excuse himself, but the jailor urged him so that he consented to tarry only a few minutes. The jailor was a communicative man. He could never rest until he had divested himself of every secret he was in possession of. Yet he was a faithful man, who might have been entrusted with the greatest treasure. He was prepared to defend the jail and environs with his life.

The jailor invited Hans to join him in a glass, at the same time opening the door of a closet. Hans consented, of course, and soon the friends were discussing upon various subjects. The conversation at length turned upon Royston, whom Hans pictured out as being one of the most abandoned men he had ever seen. The drinks were repeated, and the jailor was in a fair way of becoming intoxicated. Hans recollected that he had the piece of jewelry, which he had repaired for the jailor in his pocket. When he offered it to him, he could not be prevailed upon to receive any compensation for his work. Hans expressed a desire to see the prisoner, saying that.

as he would not be in town upon the day of the execution, he had a curiosity to see the wretch once more. The jailor consented, and led the way to his place of confinement. The massive bolts and locks yielded to the key and the pressure of the strong hand of the jailor, and they were soon in the presence of Carl Royston. The prisoner was a man above the medium size, and seemed formed for feats of strength and agility. He could not have been exceeding thirty years of age, from the appearance of his face. A heavy beard, almost jet black, corresponded with his long, flowing ringlets. There were few finer looking men than Royston. The prisoner merely bowed to Hans, as the latter, accompanied by the jailor, entered the room. Royston was seated at a table, reading a book. Several papers were scattered upon the table. Hans observed that Royston was confined by a chain, which was fastened to one of his ankles. The chain was secured by a staple driven into the floor near his bed.

Hans conversed with the prisoner upon trivial matters for some time, without alluding to the murder. Royston asked the jailor to furnish him with a supply of fresh water. While the latter was gone to get it, Hans hastily drew out the saw and a ball of twine, and gave them to Royston. He said that, upon the night previous to the day appointed for the execution, his escape must be made. The plan was imparted to Royston in a few words. The friends embraced and were silent, as they heard the footsteps of the jailor.

Hans took his departure from the jail, well pleased

with the success of his visit. The hopes of Royston
were revived. He began his work of sawing the bars
of the window, which was happily within his reach. He
worked slowly at first, and succeeded so well that the
bars were sawn sufficiently, in one night, to render them
capable of being wrenched off. The window had a
curtain, which the prisoner wisely drew over the aperture to conceal his designs. The jailor had heard no
noise, and not suspecting an attempt on the part of
the prisoner to make his escape, merely performed the
usual task of furnishing Royston with his meals. Royston concealed the saw in his bosom, resolving to part
with it only with his life.

When the jailor had performed his round, upon the
evening preceding the day set apart for the execution,
Royston commenced the task of sawing in twain the
iron that encumbered him. He labored long and diligently, and succeeded in severing it just at midnight.
He went to the window, and listened for the signal.
All was still and quiet. There was no noise in or about
the prison. His fate was in the balances, and the
weight of a feather would turn the scale. It seemed
almost an age to him when the clock tolled the hour of
one. Just then he heard a low whistle from the copse
hard by the jail-yard. He returned the signal cautiously, and applied his hands to the bars, which yielded to
his pressure. One by one they were removed. Fastening the twine to one end of the saw, Royston threw it
with all his might over the enclosure of the jail. In a
few minutes another signal was given, and he drew back

the twine and joyfully clasped the end of a rope in his
hands.   It was only the work of a few minutes to make
the cable fast to the bedstead, and swing himself from
the dizzy height to the ground.   Holding fast to the
rope, which had a fastening from without, Royston
climbed over the high wall.   He was free!

CHAPTER VIII.

WE are taught from experience. that many of the ills of life result from disappointment. When once we have placed our affections upon an object, its attainment forms our chief desire for the present moment. It matters but little how trivial is the object of our desires, the mind is not the less bent upon its pursuit. A country damsel, once upon a time, performed a journey of ten miles, on foot, to witness an execution; but the culprit was reprieved by the Governor while the Sheriff was in the act of adjusting the noose. The disappointed crowd left the place filled with regret, and the damsel sought her far-off home, bewailing her unhappy lot — complaining that Fate had decreed that she should never enjoy any of the pleasures of life!

If the execution of criminals were attended by the thoughtless thousands who witness them, with other objects than those of gratifying an idle curiosity, and of seeing the culprit enact the last scene of the drama of life, the effect upon the by-standers would be different from what it really is. The public execution of criminals was intended by our legislators, who enacted the law, to act as a warning to the people, who are never backward in crowding around the scaffold to catch the last confession of the victim of the law. Men, whose skirts were red with the blood of innocent victims, and whose hearts were black with crime, upon surveying the sympathizing crowd around them, have imagined themselves martyrs, and have died amid seeming exultations. The increase of crime has, in a measure, resulted from those *happy exits* upon the part of fiends; and many nations have substituted private for public executions.

The town of Crofton was thrown into a state of utter confusion on the morning after the escape of Royston. Five thousand persons from neighboring places were in and around Crofton, to witness the anticipated hanging. The hotels were crowded, the private houses were overflowing with visitors, and the woods were full of men, women and children, who had pitched their tents the evening before. The jailor was almost frantic when he discovered that the bird had flown. He could not conceive how the instrument had been conveyed to the prisoner. Suspicion could not rest upon Hans more than upon other men who had been admitted to Royston's cell. Besides, Hans was considered to be a man of irreproachable character. The more ignorant portion of the community imagined that Royston's escape had been effected by super-natural agency. They did not doubt but that Royston was in close league with the adversary of souls. The editor of the town paper hastened to his sanctum, locked his door to keep out intruders, seated himself by his desk, took out a fresh supply of paper, provided himself with a new pen, shook the ink, roached back his hair, crossed his legs, knit his brows, clenched his teeth, and wrote the following editorial notice:

MIRACULOUS ESCAPE!
CAPTIVUS FUGIVIT!
UNPARALLELED EXCITEMENT!
MYSTERY CONNECTED WITH IT!

"Last night, when the silvery orb had disappeared behind the horizon, and the roseate scintillations emitted from the stellated firmament alone guided mortals upon their nocturnal peregrinations, by some mysterious agency of supernal handicraft, a convicted miscreant, whose life had been forfeited to the law by disinterested and far-seeing jurors, effected his escape from *durance vile.* [Here the editor had recourse to his dictionary of quotations.] Ensconced, as he was, by the unyielding walls of the *conciergerie,* [Here the editor took snuff] manacled with a brazen chain with frequent links, guarded by day 'neath the dragon eye of the ever wakeful jailor, and by night [*tempore noctis*] by the iron doors which grate upon the brazen thresholds, how was it possible for the prisoner to have made his escape? [Here the editor coughed three times, took snuff again, and spent one hour in searching Pope's translation of the Illiad for a suitable quotation.]

'Now pleasing sleep hath closed each mortal eye,
Stretched in their tents, the Grecian leaders lie,
The immortals slumbered on their thrones above,
All but the ever-wakeful eyes of Jove.'

"Who would have supposed it within the power of one so helpless as Royston — just upon the eve of beholding, experiencing and feeling the dread realities of the unknown Future — to effect his escape from his keep, guarded by bars of triple steel. [The editor spent another hour in searching the pages of Shakspeare.]

'Ay, but to die, and go, we know not where;
To lie in cold obstruction, and to rot;'

Royston thought this, perhaps, and assisted by some elf, wrenched the mighty fabric of the windows from their strong position in the walls, and summoning all the courage his naturally brave, but depraved heart possessed, he swung down the cord, by fairies wrought, cleared the court-yard below, and vanished into thin air.

"So great is the unparalleled excitement of the infuriated crowd, that anarchy reigns without. '*Saevitque animis ignobile vulgus.*' It is apprehended, upon the part of our sooth-sayers, that '*Jamque fasces et saxa volant.*' If such a dire calamity should happen, as a natural consequence, we can only expect that '*furor arma ministrat.*' But we shall not despair. '*Nil descrandum.*'

"By the time we go to press again, we hope and fondly trust that the mystery may be cleared up. We should not be too hasty in censuring our very excellent and highly competent jailor for the escape of Carl Royston. More anon. *Nous verons.*"

The erudite editor unbolted the door of the sanctum, placed the article in the hands of the compositor, bade him use all possible dispatch, and give him a proof of it very soon.

When the paper made its appearance, the sensible portion of the citizens took a hearty laugh at the notice. Snibbens thought it was an excellent production, full of

appropriate classical quotations. It is more than probable that it saved much disturbance, as the editor himself thought, as the crowd dispersed, no lives were lost,
no blood shed, and the jailor was unmolested. *What
a powerful engine is the Press!*

The miraculous escape of Royston was the constant
theme of conversation for several days. At length the
argument was exhausted, and other topics supplied the
vacuum. The whole town was in a bustle about the approaching party at Rockford house. The merchants
were reaping a rich harvest, indeed, from the sale of
fancy goods. Blessed are those who dwell in towns,
where the bustle and confusion of a crowded and hurried
populace do not deaden the genial vitality that should
pervade society. We should live in vain, if we did not
cultivate and refine the better feelings of our nature.
If only the morbid desire of acquiring wealth, and of
elevating ourselves to a superior position in society were
the mainspring to our exertions, the world, instead of
being advanced in civilization, would cease to reflect the
light of science, and the reign of the Dark Ages would
overshadow mankind again.

By frequent repetition we are enabled to learn the
most difficult languages, and to demonstrate the most
intricate propositions. By frequent contact with our
associates we are enabled to polish our manners, and
prepare our minds for the enjoyment of that blessed
existence which is promised to the faithful. The rough

Ashlar is divested of its asperities by the art of mechanism, and prepared for the adornment of costly palaces. The golden stream of education, when left free to flow through our midst, waters and revivifies every plant in the garden of our hearts. The mind must be concentrated upon a subject before the reasoning faculties can rise superior to mere matter. It is by a strict regard to Truth, which is the touch-stone of every virtue, that society is held together—that governments flourish—and the heavenly bodies move in their accustomed sphere. Truth, like pure gold, becomes more refined by being polished; and the mind is expanded and strengthened by the force of education.

Housewives would forget the use of their utensils, if they were not, at times, permitted to bring them into requisition upon extra occasions. By the advice of aunt Margery, Mrs. Rockford ordered a complete muster of every culinary utensil upon the premises. The pots, ovens, spiders, skillets and baking-pans were all brought face to face, to give account of their stewardship. Mr. Rockford smiled to see his aunt examining the quality of every piece of ware with the care of a purchaser. After condemning about one-half the lot as unfit for service, the good dame made out a list for new articles, which were presently bought and brought into immediate requisition. All was bustle and merry confusion at Rockford house now. Turkeys were chased down, and sacrificed; chickens suffered decapitation: pigs were slaughtered; and the fish market patronized. Eggs were broken by the young ladies, and the young men lent a helping hand. Mr. Rockford pulled off his coat, laid Coke and Littleton upon the shelf, tied up his office papers securely, and followed the workers into the pastry rooms. He was soon banished from there by the edict of aunt Margery, for he had forgotten himself and upset the sugar bowls, mixed the white of the eggs with the yellow, and spoiled fully a dozen of those indispensible and ephemeral productions of the barn-yard. He had mixed the sugar and flour without waiting for commands, and must suffer banishment.

Judging that the house was almost too hot a place for him, he hastened to the yard to assist Adam and dame Phillis in roasting the meats, but he soon discovered that his presence was not required there. He attempted to turn one of the spits, and let a choice joint of meat fall into the fire.

"Dar now," said Phillis, "massa done gone spile de meat. I 'speck he done sumthin' 'rong in de hous, and missis run him out dar. Do pray, massa, go 'long to de Law offis, and leave de niggers 'lone. Dey can cook de meat better'n you."

Mr. Rockford went to the house, and vowed he would not again interfere with the arrangements of the party. He procured a list of the guests to be invited, and sent out the cards. In the meantime, the young men, who were more docile, aided the ladies in their work, and were of incalculable advantage to them. The domestic apartments were redolent with the odor of pound-cake. Every sunshiny place about the yard was put into requisition for drying the iced cake. Sebastian and Jupe

were closely guarded to keep them from mischief. Carlo
was the best custodian of the knick-knacks. The pigs
and feathered tribe, which had not been drafted, were
kept at bay by that faithful animal. He would stretch
himself out, as if asleep, by the tables, and watch the
chickens as they would step lightly upon tip-toe to per-
petrate mischief. When they were upon the point of
committing the overt act, Carlo would make an immediate sally upon them. He kept his watch faithfully,
and suffered no harm to come to the tables.

So expeditiously had the work been carried on under
the superintendence of aunt Margery, that everything
was cooked fully two days before the time appointed for
the party. She had taught Mrs. Rockford some lessons
in the art of cookery she had never known before. The
young men had labored as faithfully as any of the ca-
terers. Mr. Rockford was not allowed to go near the
pantries, for fear he might upset something. Every
apartment about the house was cleansed and put in
complete order for the reception of the guests. When
the day for the party arrived, the gentlemen took
guns, and went upon the beach to shoot gulls and ducks.
Aunt Margery sat down to crimp the border of her new
cap. Mrs. Rockford was busy in performing a thousand useless things, but anything to keep the mind
employed is better than to sit down and do nothing.
Miss Frances took Sebastian and Jupe, and went to
play. Carlo kept guard at the entrance of the dining-
room. The numerous cats and pigeons about the premises were not too good to displace many a thing and

spoil it. Miss Roxana Fairfield, who had a mind of a literary caste, sat down to write a letter to one of her female friends in Colonna. As we have the liberty, let us look over her shoulder while she writes. It is said that time discovers all things; let us rather take it by the fore-lock in this instance.

But, gentle reader, do not imagine that you are doing a very praise-worthy action in prying into the secrets of others. If you can keep your own, it is well; but it is almost impossible for you to keep those of your friends. There are really but few secrets kept. You may trace out, by enquiry, a solution almost to everything. But let us give everything its due. There is a society existing among us which has kept secrets from time immemorial. The very actions of Solomon and his wise men are known to that society, and even to its neophytes. Who will say that mankind is unfaithful, when MASONRY has withstood the ravages of time? But, by Miss Roxana's leave, we will look over her shoulder as she writes. It may throw some light upon our novel.

"ROCKFORD HOUSE, April 15th, 18—.

"*Dear Helen :*—When I left our beautiful town of Colonna, only three weeks since, you exacted a promise from me that I would write you often, if my stay at Rockford house should be prolonged. I trust you will excuse me, my dear friend, when I confess to you that since my arrival at this romantic place, my mind has been so occupied by the sight of new scenes, which are truly enchanting, that I have been seemingly derelict in the performance of sacred duties. Upon this beautiful morning, which bids fair to be the happiest day of my life, I am seated in my well furnished apartment, writing to you, my dear Helen, who have shared my bliss and divided my sorrows from our early childhood. The window of my apartment commands a fine view of the Atlantic, and I can distinctly see the briny billows as they chase each other to the beach. Mr. Rockford and our male friends, who attended us here, are out upon the beach, waging war upon the gulls and ducks. The report of their fowling-pieces is distinctly heard every few minutes.

"To-night we are to have a grand party; but I shall not anticipate. It may not be uninteresting to you to have a short rehearsal of every thing we have done, seen and heard since we left Colonna.

"We women are such queer creatures, that we are not satisfied with an outline; we must have the particulars of every scene. You shall not be deprived of that pleasure, dearest, if what I write may convey to you a faint idea of our trip to this place, and what we have been doing since our arrival. You remember, Helen, how we were amused at the exhibitions of a magician, who came to Colonna several years ago; and with what rapidity he changed and varied his performances? How we clapped our hands and laughed, and were almost dizzy at beholding the extraordinary feats of his magic lantern? It is true they were simple enough, and could have been performed by almost any skillful man, yet first impressions are the most lasting, and we have ever considered Mons. De Luce as the greatest man we have ever seen. My mind has been a mirror of late, upon which many scenes have been reflected. You need not prepare yourself to read a secret, my friend, for you are aware that I am not fond of telling them.

"But to begin with the beginning. I believe you have never traveled from Colonna to this plase. A description of the trip may help me to fill up the sheet; for I do abhor the idea of sending a letter to a correspondent only half filled up. I can judge from my own feelings. It irates me to receive only a few hurried lines from a dear friend. I feel like re-enclosing a short, uninteresting epistle to the author. But I shall not keep you in suspense.

Our trunks were packed with as much care as we usually bestow upon such matters, (and you know, Helen, you and I have spent three blessed days in packing our trunks, when we were upon the point of leaving our homes to go to college,) and, all things having been prepared for our departure, my dear mother, sister Fannie and your tormentor were politely handed into the family carriage by the very kind Mr. Watson and your waggish friend, Mr. Judson. Those worthy young men had accepted of an invitation from mother to be our attendants. They followed our carriage in a buggy, and we left the village of Colonna with joyful hearts. We had not been from home in a long time, and, to confess the truth, I had become so heartily tired out with Colonna, that I had arrived at the same conclusion with Alexander Selkirk,

'It is better to dwell in the midst of alarms,
Than to reign in this horrible place.'
6

"Do not suppose, dearest, that I wish to cast any aspersions upon the fame of our town. Far from it; but I longed to behold other scenes, and I left my home with a joyful heart. We were soon out of Colonna, and were passing through a beautiful country. The high, sandy ridges were densely covered with the tall, stately pines. As I leaned my head out of the window of the carriage, and listened to the mournful sighing of those Leviathans of the forest, I became almost sad; but then they are crowned with foliage all the year round, and look so beautiful, especially in the Spring, when they put on a new dress. Their tasselated leaves do not wither, but at the appointed time they are forced to give place to the younger shoot.

"You have no idea, dearest Helen, how many beautiful streams we crossed. We could see the fish playing upon the pebbly beds. When we would get out at such places to rest the horses, we would cast pebbles at the fish. They would dart off under their retreat at the bank, but when we threw them some crumbs, they would come very near us. One large trout came to the surface to get a chicken bone which Fannie threw into the stream, when Mr. Judson, who is never better employed than when engaged in sport, gave him so severe a blow with the big end of his whip, that the scaly victim was killed outright.

"We passed many fine residences. I was surprised to see so much magnificence displayed in the country. Those who reside in such lovely retreats, with every convenience around them, should never despair of en-

joyment. If I could exchange my residence in Colonna
for a retreat, like some I saw when I came to this place.
I could spend my life so pleasantly.

"By eleven o'clock in the morning, we arrived at Mr.
Rockford's stately mansion, having left Colonna at sun-
rise. We were scarcely six hours upon the road, though
our speed had not been great. But you know how very
careful mother is of her horses. She would not travel
more than four miles an hour to gratify us or any person else. Mr. Rockford came and welcomed us with
such a becoming grace, and his wife has been so agreeable, that I shall be sorry when the time comes for us to
return to Colonna.

"We have had delightful drives about the town, and
pleasant excursions in the sail-boats. Numerous friends
have called to see us, and we have repaid their visits.
I wish you could see Sebastian Rockford! He is one of
the prettiest boys I have ever beheld. He is truly and
wonderfully intelligent. His parents love him so fondly
that I am afraid something will happen to the child.
But what a foolish saying that is, Helen, as if the love
one bears to a child should not rather be a protection
than a misfortune.

"I have almost filled my sheet, yet I have told you
only a few of the many things I have seen. As I inti-
mitated to you, in the beginning of this letter, that we
were to have a magnificent party to-night in honor of our
visit, please allow me to put a period to this hastily
written letter. If I am not too much fatigued, I will
write you again to-morrow.

"In the mean time, dearest, think of me as your very
especial friend, ROXANA FAIRFIELD."

CHAPTER IX.

When Mr. Rockford and his two friends had filled their game-bags with as many birds as they chose to carry, they directed their steps homeward, well pleased with the morning's sport. There are many birds to be found upon the sea-shore which can be scarcely ranked among the aquatic tribe. They not unfrequently wage war with the Grallatores, which, after wading into the water and capturing their prey, are ruthlessly deprived of the proceeds of their labor. The Snipe, the smallest species of the Grallatores, is a timid and cautious bird. The slightest motion of the hunter will cause it to seek safety in flight. Some bird-hunters suppose that the old flint and steel lock guns are not quick enough in exploding to kill them. Be that as it may, they are not easily bagged. The Partridge, of the order Gallinæ, family Tetraonidæ, are generally found in low countries. They resemble our barn-yard fowl, are war-like in their disposition, attacking any animal which may disturb their young. They are generally shot upon the wing by sportsmen, who train their pointers to the task of flushing them. They go in flocks, and, except in the laying season, when they are only found in pairs, fifty or sixty may be seen in one flock. They are fond of grain; but, like other birds, are equally satisfied with

insects. Their flesh is sweet and wholesome, and he is
no Epicure who refuses a roasted Partridge.

The bags of the huntsmen were filled with Ducks and
Partridges, with a few Woodcocks and Snipes.

"Here are some delicacies, Josephine," said Mr.
Rockford. "Have a few of the choice birds served up
for dinner."

"Your success has been commensurate with your desires, one would think, from the great number of the
feathered tribe you have slain," said Miss Roxana to
Mr. Watson.

"Indeed, madam," replied the gallant, "we have not
sported this morning to no purpose. I have scarcely
ever seen birds more plentiful. We took our stations,
hidden from view by the copse, and when a Duck would
light near us, Mr. Rockford would request one of us to
shoot it, and enjoin upon the other to be ready to fire
upon the birds on shore, which, of a surety, were concealed all around us in clusters."

Here an interesting lecture upon the subject of orni-
thology, by Mr. Rockford, occupied the time that intervened until the dinner hour. When that meal had been
duly discussed, the friends separated, to meet no more
until the arrival of the guests for the party.

At the usual hour for fashionable gatherings to con-
vene, the extensive parlors and reception rooms were
crowded with the numerous guests. Every one in the
town, who made any pretensions to gentility, was invited. If any deserving persons had been neglected, it
was not the fault of the Rockfords. The fashionable.

the gay and the grave were represented. The aged
attended their children, to see them duly initiated into
the mysteries of fashionable society. The belles of the
town were dressed in the finest silks, satins and embroidered muslins. Those maidens, to whom Nature
had not been so lavish of its charms, supplied the de-
fects by the beautiful colors of the toilet-box.

When Josephus Napoleon Bonaparte Snibbens conducted Miss Jerusha Smith into the parlor, nothing but
good breeding prevented an outburst of laughter. The
appearance of this strange couple was anything but
prepossessing. Miss Jerusha was very stately, being
several inches taller in person than her pedantic escort.
The superfluity of bows, flounces and laces of her dress,
did not fail to attract the attention of those, even, who
were not connoisseurs in the art of haberdashery. Like
some jewellers, who seek to make a display by wearing
numberless rings and pins, Miss Jerusha, who was a
milliner, had surely made herself, upon that occasion,
a locomotive sign post for the display of her goods.
Mr. Snibbens had been studying the costume, as well as
the attitude of the first Napoleon. Buff pants, a vest
of the same material, and a blue frock coat, cut in the
true military style, and fastened in front with military
buttons, set off the figure of the namesake of the "little
corporal." Snibbens seated his charge, and commenced
discoursing his acquaintances upon abstruse sciences
generally.

Conversation soon became general, and the modest
reserve that naturally restrains the guests when they

first enter a parlor, gave place to fluent discourse. Samuel Culverhouse and his ancient spouse were there, prepared to listen to the conversation of the guests of their own age, and to collect all the little news items that were afloat in the town. Samuel and Dorothy were an amiable, but homely couple. As a certain wag has facetiously said, *those two made a pair.* Samuel's blue domestic suit, which had only been worn seventeen years, appeared to rather better advantage upon that occasion than usual, thanks to the renovating ordeal that all household goods were subjected to by the excellent Dorothy. She never permitted anything to go to waste about her; far from it. She had taken off the fourteen yard border of her antique cap, washed it in milk-warm water with a little weak soap, carried it through a course of mysteries, quilled it up, as she had done an hundred times before, and sewed it back again. Her silver spectacles, with the large circular glasses never became her better than they did on the night of the party. She held in her hand a large turkey-tail fan, bound with blue morocco. The good old couple said but few words, but they were busily compiling information to be used on future occasions, perhaps at the breakfast table on the next morning.

The Misses Fairfield were arrayed in costly but plain dresses, and received an abundance of attention from the young gentlemen. Their good sense and fine accomplishments fitted them for the adornment of the most polite and elegant circles in which they had been accustomed to move. The grace with which they received the addresses of their friends, might be attributed to the excellent training they had received from their parents. One of the young men, who was conversing with Miss Roxana, escorted her to the piano. While the company was entertained by the music, several interesting scenes were being enacted in the room. An old gentleman, who was noted for his wealth, had two daughters present. The Misses Slocum were the belles of Crofton, and were as much sought after for their wealth as for any accomplishments they possessed. Mr. Slocum was very corpulent, and his manners exceedingly stiff and starchy. His daughters were obedient disciples, and early imbibed the exalted notions of their parents. The young men of Crofton, who were not wealthy, were not welcome guests at Slocum hall. Slocum had instructed his daughters, before arriving at Mr. Rockford's, not to receive any advances from young lawyer Spingles, or from Dr. Montague, as they were both very poor. He had never been pleased with their visits to his house. When he took his seat, and observed that both of the young men named were present, he felt disquieted. He enjoined upon his wife the necessity of keeping a strict surveillance over Amelia and Julia during the evening. He was not kept long in suspense, for Spingles was casting furtive glances in the direction of the Slocum circle. Miss Amelia reddened, her father grew angry, and her mother darted basilisk glances at Spingles.

"Here he comes, wife," said Slocum. "Just leave him to me. I will not let him enjoy the company of our daughter very long."

Spingles, who was a young man of sterling worth, but poor and proud, now approached and saluted each member of the Slocum family, and seated himself beside Miss Amelia. He had scarcely passed the compliments of the evening, when Slocum, after having made an attack upon his gold snuff-box, which he never neglected to display upon all occasions, addressed Spingles after the following style:

"You have only been residing in the town a few years, I believe, Mr. Spingles?"

"Four years next Fall," said the young man.

"Where did you graduate, sir? My sons all graduated at Yale College," rejoined the irated Slocum.

"Indeed, sir," replied Spingles, "I must confess that I had not the advantages of a collegiate course."

"Pity, pity, sir; but you cannot expect to arrive at distinction. A young man without wealth, or the prestige of family influence, cannot aspire to lofty positions in society."

"Truly, sir," said Spingles, "I am at a loss to comprehend you. I cannot believe that you desire to offend me, but your conversation has assumed a strange form for a social circle. I despise the aristocracy of wealth, or the false position a young man tries to assume by the aid of family influence. If your remarks are intended to apply to my penniless circumstances, I must ask the pardon of your exalted reverence, promising not again to place myself in a position to receive an affront from an ill-mannered aristocrat."

Slocum was nonplussed. He endeavored to explain.

but the young man turned a deaf ear to his confused apology, and passed into another circle. The Slocums did not enjoy themselves as well as they anticipated, as they screened themselves from the contact of *their inferiors :* their equals (in wealth) had but little to gain in seeking their confidence.

Mr. Rockford and his good lady passed from room to room, endeavoring to render their guests comfortable and entirely at home. Watson and Judson were delighted with the pleasant company. They proved themselves particularly interesting to several young ladies, whose acquaintance they had formed several days before. Aunt Margery gave entertainment to the old folks, who chiefly assembled in a parlor apart from the gay young men and women. Sebastian, and a few juveniles, enjoyed themselves in the nursery, as the mother had set a table there for their especial benefit.

Rockford house was indeed filled with merriment. The long piazza was crowded with promenaders, who chose to pass an hour thus in social chit-chat. The moon shone brightly upon some who stepped out upon the terrace to pluck a flower, or to whisper the soft words of first love.

"Time flew by on golden winglets," and still pleasure fanned the cheek of every one that sought it. The haughty few, who threw themselves upon their dignity, as was the custom of the Slocums, were almost entirely overlooked and neglected. Some gathered around the chess and whist tables, others engaged in lively conversation. Snibbens let off superfluous quantities of gas.

to the edification of some, but to the amusement or disgust of the more refined. The old folks heartily longed for supper time to come. Samuel and Dorothy were anxious to see the table, and the former fully intended to do the subject full justice.

It was whispered around that there would be a *surprise*, as they termed it, immediately after supper, but it was not ascertained what the performance would consist of. Every one was in suspense, when the announcement for supper was made. There was a general rush for partners, and the long hall was crowded almost to suffocation. When the magnificent feast was concluded and the company had repaired to the parlors again, Mr. Rockford invited the ladies to walk up to the rooms upon the second floor.

Mr. Rockford was rather opposed to making an aristocratic display upon any occasion, but he wished to amuse his guests. He had invited a few select and tasty friends, of both sexes, to his house, a few days before the party, and they had gotten up some tableaux and charades. After two or three rehearsals, they were prepared for the representation. A temporary stage, some scenery and a drop-curtain were prepared.

Tableaux-vivants! What could it mean? asked a hundred persons of Snibbens, who was the oracle of a certain class in the town. Snibbens had not "looked out" the word, and was at his row's end. He scratched his head, bit his pale lips, and said nothing. One of the young men supposed it meant table-turning, or something of that kind, he was not exactly certain. Uncle

Samuel told them they would learn what it meant by waiting, as he was sure Mr. Rockford meant not only to amuse, but to instruct them. Dorothy, having drank five or six glasses of wine and syllabub, fell fast asleep, supported by the stalwart arm of her husband. At length the curtain rose, and revealed an interesting group. An officer, rather beyond the prime of life, stood gazing at a departing ship. Several were looking upon him with sorrowful countenances. A harpist reclined upon his instrument; several attendants were represented as weeping. The tableau was complete: the curtain dropped. It was Napoleon at the island of St. Helena. Snibbens was charmed. He recognized the god of his adoration. He had overheard a gentleman tell another the meaning of "tableaux-vivants," and he was now explaining it to several around him.

The curtain rose again and revealed the inside of a prison. A tall, finely formed man, dressed in the costume of the Elizabethan age, was clasping the hands of a lady, and imprinting a kiss upon her brow. The sullen warden held the massive bunch of keys in one hand, and beheld the scene with feelings of indifference. A file of soldiers awaited without, holding their muskets, with match-locks, prepared for any emergencies. The fetters had been taken from the ankles of the distinguished personage, but his wrists were secured with a chain. His manuscripts and books revealed his studious habits. The taper was burning at his table. It was Sir Walter Raleigh taking leave of his wife on the morning of his execution.

After the performers had exhibited quite a number of excellent tableaux, Mr. Rockford announced that a few charades or rebuses would be represented. While the company were waiting for the curtain to rise, the orchestra discoursed sweet music. There is nothing so acceptable as music when the mind is free from care; there is nothing so soothing as music when the mind is troubled with care. Let the dulcet strains of an Æolian harp, or the wild warbling notes of an inspired child of song lull us to slumber, when our souls are sad.

The curtain rose again. A triumphal arch, covered with roses and vines, was on the stand. A conqueror passed under it. while the ladies and children threw garlands at his feet. The scene was changed, and a group of shepherds, in oriental costume, appeared. They conversed apart, as if expecting something wonderful to happen. They had heard some Heavenly music, and expected a vision. Suddenly a crimson light flashed across the stage, and an *angel* appeared. The shepherds fled, and the scene closed. *Archangel* was the subject.

Many were the representations, and the company dispersed not until the small hours warned them to seek their homes. The party was pronounced, by every one, to be a decided success. All who were present wished a long and happy life to Mr. Rockford, whose chief delight appeared to be that of dispelling sorrows, and dispensing blessings upon his race.

He is a noble benefactor, who, instead of sinking his friends in the sea of trouble, will take them by the hand

and lift them to his own level. Remember, kind reader, you were sent to bless, not to curse mankind. This
is a moving world, and the scenes are ever changing.
You can not remain an idle spectator, while the drama
of life is performed. You must stem the tide, or the
current may bear you off.

CHAPTER X.

A few days subsequent to the party, aunt Margery and her company bade adieu to the good folks of Rockford house, and sought the pleasant town of Colonna, having been absent from their home much longer than they anticipated. Quiet was again restored to the town of Crofton. The escape of Royston had given place to the week's conversation to which Rockford festival had given rise. There was nothing out of the routine of the ordinary affairs of life, worthy of notice, in the place for several weeks. At length, Hans Kremple received a letter without a signature, but he knew from a glance that Royston was the author of it. We take the liberty of laying the contents of the letter before our readers:

"POINT PEAK, May 10th, 18—.

"*Dear Hans:*—I am here, in this sylvan retreat, enjoying the beautiful scenery and as many of the luxuries of life as I wish, for the present. The close confinement of the prison had almost wrecked my constitution; but, thanks to the salubrious atmosphere of this healthy retreat, I have regained my accustomed strength. It is true, that I am indebted to you for the fortunate escape I made from confinement. The saw you gave me performed the task most admirably, and indeed you played your part with much tact, or I should not now be permitted to write this letter to you.

"When I parted with you on that eventful night, I followed the directions you gave me, and found jolly Ben awaiting my arrival with much anxiety. I sprang upon the horse he had prepared for me, and we were soon beyond the vicinity of a place which had but few charms for me. It was broad daylight when we arrived at Hermit's Retreat. Our friends were expecting me, and were prepared to face any danger that might present itself on my account. The tears stole down my own cheeks, as I beheld them weep at once more beholding me. They pressed around and embraced me, and almost devoured me with kind offices.

"I dispatched a hasty meal, changed my apparel, received a supply of gold from the strong box, had my hair and whiskers curtailed, and mounted my black charger and left my friends, to seek the covert of some wild retreat. I am fully one hundred miles from you. but at present it is not exactly prudent for any of our men to come here. I am spending my time at the house of a good farmer, who has taken quite a fancy to me. You would laugh at me, were I to tell you under what name I am known to him. My profession or avocation suits me as well as yours does you. I can tune pianos and perform upon several instruments nearly as well as you can repair watches or make *saws*.

"Do go to our friends and tell them I am safe. When the officers shall have quit scouring the country for me. then I may pay them a visit. I have read my description in several papers which the old farmer brings home with him from the rural post-office. I wear those spectacles you gave me, and if you were to meet me upon the highway, it is not probable that you would recognize your leader.

"The killing of Winslow has placed a heavier burden upon my soul than any crime I ever committed; yet I owe Rockford a grudge. He shall yet have cause to remember Carl Royston.

"When I write you again, you shall have a description of my present retreat. You must not laugh at me, Hans, for counterfeiting an honest occupation. I prefer to undergo even the hardest labor imaginable, to remaining in a close prison. Who would be deprived of the skies one hour, if within his power to be free? We have lakes and small streams here, filled with an abundance of fish. The scenery around my retreat here, is wild and beautiful. The hills are elevated almost to the height of mountains. I am enjoying myself as well as I ever did. I am almost tempted, sometimes, to cut the acquaintance of such scape graces as you and Heinrich; but then I know that you would get yourselves into scrapes you could never be extricated from without my assistance. Do not fear treachery from me. I shall prove true to the end. Caution the boys to make no more sallies in the direction of Crofton until I come among them. Address me at Point Peak, as Monsieur Henri Deveaux, as that is my assumed name."

When Hans read the letter, he smiled, and seemed much pleased at the news it contained. He sought out

Heinrich, who had an office not far from his own. Heinrich was ostensibly a painter, but his employees performed more work than he did. He was dispatched to the retreat to convey the information that Royston was safe, and would be with them at no distant day.

Han Kremple was a jolly fellow, who might have been a good citizen and a useful man, but fate had early decreed that he should be a thief. He had so early forgotten the distinction between his own goods and those of his neighbors, that he had arrived at the conclusion that what he filched from those who could afford to lose it, if applied to good purposes, amounted to no crime. It was through his instrumentality that Royston had been seduced from his upright course, and made the intrepid leader of a lawless band of robbers. Heinrich was another young man, whom the influences of Hans had beguiled into evil habits.

So well concealed had been the manœuvres of these lawless wights, that suspicion had not even rested upon them. Indeed, so contrary was the sentiment of the citizens of Crofton, as related to the fidelity of Hans, that he was generally considered to be a man of strict honesty. Upon one occasion, when he was returning from a peddling tour, he entered the town and reported that a band of robbers had waylaid and robbed him of some of his wares. No fox, that ever escaped the huntsman by artifice, had more cunningly devised plans than Hans had.

He frequently reported skirmishes that the citizens of the community had had with the banditti, but, under his lead, the officers of the law were always led in the direction contrary to the place of hostilities.

Hans had the happy faculty of attending parties, and making himself perfectly agreeable. He prided himself upon being a judge of jewelry, but not being contented to risk his judgment at a hasty glance, it was natural for him to take several silver forks and spoons home with him from those parties, to put them to a strict test. He was never known to return them to their right owners. It arose, probably, from his being very absent minded. Taken all in all, Hans was a rare genius. You might travel over two continents without finding his equal. He reminded one of the prig, Sir Walter Scott described as being a man with so generous a heart, that he stole a quantity of clothes to keep the moths from eating them. Hans kept a fine store, and many customers flocked to it to purchase fine wares, and have their jewelry repaired. If some of them recognized matches to lost spoons, forks and silver cups, oh! indulgent reader, do not impute it to any thing but chance.

But as some authors have said, that there are no things similar or like unto each other, except the *same*, we may at once infer that the philosophy of *chance* is at an end when brought to bear upon the actions of Hans. At any rate, by artifice and cunning, he managed to live above suspicion.

He pondered several days upon the reply it behooved him to return to the communication he had received from Royston, and, after torturing his brain for a suitable answer, the following was agreed upon:

"CROFTON, May 15th, 18—.

"*Dear Carl:*—I was beginning to be low in spirits in regard to your safety and welfare, when the post brought me your very acceptable letter. I could scarcely conceive, however, that one so accustomed to the ways of the world as you are, should be at a loss, for a moment, how to steer his bark. I sometimes feel the goadings of conscience, upon reflecting that I am the chief instrument of your ruin; but, then, every action is not viewed through the same medium. What is termed honesty with some men, is downright villainy with others. I have been led to believe that the right of property consists, in a great degree, in the strongest owner. What you, or others, think in relation to the same, is only a difference of opinion, and you are entitled to your judgment.

"The town is perfectly quiet in regard to your escape, you may believe. I was not in town when the news was circulated; but upon my arrival, the day after, I raised a squad of men, who scoured the country in the portion that it was morally certain you had not gone to. Rest assured of one thing: that your friends here will use every exertion to keep your retreat an entire secret from the beagles of the law.

"There was a grand demonstration at the house of your enemy only a few days since. The whole party-going population of the place had an invitation to the party. That the affair was a magnificent one, none can doubt. Such a programme was never enacted before in this place. You know me too well to believe that I let an opportunity slip of adding a few things to my common stock. It cost me only a few strokes of the scraper to efface the name of Rockford from several fine articles of great value. I sold one piece of silver that found a lodgment in one of my pockets upon that memorable night, for enough to maintain your humble servant a long time.

"I shall expect to hear from you again at no very distant day. In the meantime, believe me,

"Yours very sincerely,

"HANS KREMPLE."

For the space of several months, the officers of justice were upon the alert to discover the lurking place of the fugitive; but so well had the whole affair been managed, it was firmly believed that he had fled from the country. If suspicion had rested upon the robbers (whom the best laid stratagems had, as yet, failed to entrap) as affording an asylum to the convicted felon, that suspicion only aroused those lawless men to greater vigilance in eluding pursuit. Hans took it into his head to go and see his friends at Hermit's Retreat. He had been denied that privilege so long, that the company of honest men had become irksome to him. He was soon provided with a vehicle capable of conveying whatever articles of merchandise he thought proper to sell as he traveled. He journeyed for a few miles upon a road not likely to conduct him to the Hermit's Retreat, but, like a cunning fox, he soon changed his course, and arrived safely at the place of his destination in a few hours.

The appearance of the house was by no means prepossessing, nor was it remarkable for huge proportions or elegance of structure. It had only six rooms, and, to all appearances, it was the residence of an unpretending farmer, or a country hotel. "Hilton House" was the rude sign that vibrated at the pleasure of the wind. Dame Elspeth and her husband were the ostensible proprietors, the former taking almost the entire charge of the business. When Hans drove up and alighted from his vehicle, dame Elspeth, who was a tidy, smart old woman, adjusted her spectacles, and surveyed the newcomer with a very scrutinizing glance. When she recognized him, her countenance cleared up, and she hastened to welcome him.

"Why, bless your body, Hans, is it really you that's come this way once more? It's truly a long time since a body has seen ye. I was sure some one was coming, for my nose has been itching the blessed day."

Hans was ushered into the reception room, and Elspeth prepared for him a hasty, though well served repast. Dandie Doane, the husband of Elspeth, soon came in from his work, and informed Hans that six of the friends had been absent a few days, but were expected at home that evening. If they should prove successful in their operations, it was more than probable they would return laden with rich booty.

Dandie's declarations were shortly verified by the arrival of several men on horseback, followed by a wagon, which was drawn by two stout horses. The driver had all the appearance of a country lout returning from market with his year's supplies, but a person versed in physiognomy would have arrived at a different conclusion. The whole group presented a motley appearance indeed ; but when they recognized Hans, they threw off their reserve and appeared in their true character. Ben Harley was the leader of this lawless band of men in the absence of Royston. He was a man above the medium size, thick set and well muscled. His face and care-worn brow indicated that he had passed the meridian of life. His long, bushy beard and dark, flowing hair gave him a remarkable appearance, and his black, sparkling eye was sufficient of itself to designate him as a bold, dauntless man.

It was night, and the sable curtains were drawn darkly around "Hilton House." Dandie Doane and dame Elspeth spread the festive board in one of the rooms remote from intrusion. The old folks, at the command of Ben Harley, brought out the wines and several kinds of stronger spirituous liquors, and retired to keep watch. After several glasses had been drunk by the company, Ben commanded three of the men to look after the goods they had taken, and have them conveyed quietly to the cave, and to remove every appearance and vestige of their arrival. Two of the more trusty men were permitted to remain with him and Hans, as the latter was a confidential friend of the gang whose society they seldom enjoyed.

"Come, Ben," said Hans, " you have often promised to relate your adventures to me, but it has never been entirely convenient until now. Will you not gratify me this time—it will help to while away an hour so pleasantly ? "

CHAPTER XI.

First outlaw.—" Fellows, stand fast ; I see a prisoner."
Second outlaw.—" If there be ten, shrink not, but down with 'em."
              Enter Valentine and Speed.
Third outlaw.—" Stand, sir, and throw us that you have about you ;
if not, we'll make you sit, and rifle you."
Speed—" Sir, we are undone ! these are the villains that all the trav-
elers do fear so much."

Two Gentlemen of Verona.

BEING thus importuned, Ben Harley arose from his
seat and went to the door ; and having satisfied himself
that no eaves-dropper was lurking around the house, he
brought both the lock and the bolt into requisition to
prevent a surprise.   He drank another glass of brandy,
and resuming his seat at the table, thus began :

" You must prepare your mind, dear Hans, to hear
no maiden's story.   My father resided in this State,
and was surrounded with the comforts if not the luxuries
of life.   He was kind and indulgent to his servants,
and my brothers seemed to possess his love in so great
a degree, that their presence was indispensable to his
happiness.   But, strange to say, he conceived a dislike
to me almost from the hour of my birth, as my mother
informed me ; and I have feeling recollections of having
received unmerciful castigations from his hands ere I
had arrived at the age of discerning right from wrong.

Well do I remember the stern looks and cruel reproofs he bestowed upon my mother, when, almost frantic, she rescued me from his clutches. Yet was I gentle and obedient to the tyrant ; never daring to speak to him except when interrogated. My mother was my only friend. Without the angelic love she manifested for me, and the matronly care she bestowed upon me when not restrained by her husband, my slender frame would have reposed beneath the sod of the church yard ere I had passed my first decade. My brothers hated me from the sympathy they possessed for our father, whose love they had never divided with me. I was the unfortunate recipient of their unremitting abuses, and they compelled me to carry their books to and from school as if I had been a hired servant. I complained to my mother of their unnatural treatment, but received only her tears for consolation, with a promise that she would entreat my father to intercede in my behalf. Instead of an amelioration of the unfraternal manner in which my brothers acted towards me, it really seemed as if they were bent upon my destruction.

"It is an old adage, and a true one, that ' a hair will break a camel's back.' I had borne the insults, kicks and rebuffs of those graceless boys so long, that I was determined to be submissive no more. My heart sank within me, and I was almost frantic with grief ; and if I could not place a period to our unhappy intercourse, I was fully prepared to make the effort and abide the consequences. One evening, we had scarcely left the old rustic school house on our return home, when my tormentors insisted upon loading me, as usual, with their books and buckets, avowing that they desired to play at hide-and-seek among the huge pines and oaks that shaded the grove through which our path led. I demurred to their injunctions and positively refused to accommodate them. They commenced an abusive tirade against me. I retorted, and my courage soon rose to fever heat. The trio came at me under full charge, but I parried their blows, returning several well aimed strokes with my slate. I succeeded in keeping them at bay until several of our fellow students came to my rescue. I had almost killed my brother George by an unlucky stroke of the slate, whose edges had been deprived of the frame during the encounter.

The blood was streaming from a severe wound upon his head, when my father came up. My brother was conveyed home almost senseless. I sought the protection of my mother, believing that my father would never listen at my version of the unfortunate difficulty. I was not kept long in suspense. My father searched for and found the instrument of torture, which was a huge leathern whip. I was dragged, nearer dead than alive, from the protection of my only friend, and made to endure the strokes of the whip, until I sank upon the floor perfectly senseless. When I revived, I was lying upon my trundle bed, and my mother was bending over me, weeping bitterly. After satisfying herself that I was out of danger, she imprinted a sweet kiss upon my burning lips, and bidding me good night, departed to the privacy of her own chamber.

My resolution was soon formed. The candle my sainted mother had left upon the table, was yet burning. I rose and listened. All was quiet in the house. I slipped easily upon tip-toe to the chamber of my brothers, who slept in the room adjoining mine. I crept to the bed, and by the light of the moon which shone into the room, I discovered that George slept sweetly. His head was bound up, but from the regularity of his breathing, and from the absence of fever as indicated by the feelivg of his hand, I was certain that he was out of danger. I kissed him tenderly as he he slept, and goin to the couch of my two youngest brothers, I performed the same kind office for them and crept back to my room.

"I was not long in forming a bundle of some of my clothes. I extinguished the light, and stealing softly through the parlor, I left the house of my father, not knowing when I should again return.

"Years passed, and I had traveled over many States. I had grown up almost a vagrant. I had been a sailor. Our ship was taken by pirates, and by chance I alone was saved, while my companions were forced to walk the fatal plank. Oh! I shall never forget how their piteous screams pierced my ears as they struggled with the devouring waves, which swallowed them as they cried for mercy. I supposed that my fate would even be worse than that of my lost companions, but I was presently informed that if I would swear fidelity to them, and become a pirate, my life should be spared. Those terms were presently complied with. They were

Spaniards and French; the captain having been born at Marseilles. I had learned a smattering of those languages before, but in a few weeks I could converse with fluency in both.

"I spent several years with these lawless infidels, and in faith, I had become so habituated to crime, that I could draw a cutlas across the throat of a prisoner with as much complaisance as any pirate that ever unfurled his black flag upon the dark blue waters of the tempestuous Mediterranean. Every enterprise must have an end, and all evil doers, must, sooner or later, meet with the condign punishment that is merited by their crimes. Our captain was the most heartless wretch that ever walked the deck of a piratical sloop. If he took a notion to seize a vessel with grappling irons, preparatory to boarding it, no person could persuade him to desist from his perilous undertaking.

"He ordered us one day to board a vessel which was in pursuit of us. We begged, entreated and implored him to crowd on the sails and seek safety in flight. He drew his pistols from his broad belt, and threatend to shoot any pirate who should disobey his orders. We submitted; and waiting until the vessel was near enough to claim *us* as a prize, we poured one broad-side into it. The cracking of masts, and the screams of the wounded were heard, and before the smoke cleared away, we were upon the deck, making havoc with all those we encountered. Our captain was contending in a hand-to-hand fight with an elderly man, whose strength was fast giving way. What was my astonishment when I recognized in the person of the old man, whose life was suspended as if by a hair, my father, whose form I had not seen since the night he inflicted the unmerited castigation upon me.

"I rushed to his side, and implored the pirate to spare my father's life. He did not heed me, but, redoubling his exertions, disarmed my father, and laid him prostrate and bleeding upon the deck. So quickly was the work accomplished, that my interference in my father's behalf was ineffectual. I drew a pistol from my belt, and shot the cruel pirate through the heart. He fell and expired without a groan. I bent over the bleeding form of my father, and discovered that he was not dead. By the assistance of one of the pirates, who had ever been a friend to me, my father was removed to a place of safety. Hurrying back to the deck, I perceived that the pirates had slain nearly all of the opposing combatants.

"Great was the consternation of the pirates when they beheld their beloved, yet tyrannical captain lying stark and stiff in the cold embraces of death. I fondly hoped that no positive evidence would convict me of the wanton deed ; yet I trembled at the result. When quiet had been restored, and the body of our captain conveyed to his state-room, I summonded the crew, and revealed to them that my father was lying *in articulo mortis* upon the deck of the captured vessel. They were moved at my immoderate grief, and yielded to my supplications. My dying parent was removed to a comfortable room upon our vessel. He was much revived by the kindly aid we afforded him, but why delay the fact? he died in a few hours.

"He was much affected when I made myself known to him, and fondly prayed that I would forgive him for the cruel treatment he had heaped upon me. Late at night our captain was lowered to the depths of the sea. I implored my friends to permit me to behold the face of my parent until a few short hours should have elapsed before consigning it to the watery grave.

"We were only a few leagues from shore, and I resolved to take my friend, and, in the stillness of the night, when the pirates, as was their custom, should betake themselves to deep drinking and be quieted into profound sleep by too frequent draughts from the festive bowl, leave forever the sickening scenes, and take my father's remains with me. Pierre assented to every proposition I made, and while our comrades were jubilant over the victories of the day, and were dividing the booty, we were silently making preparations for our escape when first an opportunity should present itself. The grief at the loss of my father, and the known attachment of Pierre to me, were a sufficient excuse for our absence from the banquet.

"As we had surmised, it was scarcely midnight when the revelry almost totally subsided; and soon after, the only noise we heard was the dashing of the waves against the vessel. The moon had just risen in all its splendor, and the stars paled before the majestic queen of night. We quietly visited every portion of the vessel. Every one was locked in the embraces of Mor-

pheus. The night-watch had yielded to the potent influences of the wines. We hastily exchanged our sailor's
garb for citizen's costume, and collecting supplies of
provisions, and as much gold and silver coin as we could
find, we lowered our cargo, together with the body of
my deceased father, into one of the boats, and leaving
the vessel to which we had been attached for so many
years, we were soon drifting upon the waves of the Atlantic.

"Guided by the moon and stars, which are unerring
guides to experienced sailors, we directed our course to
the shore. When day dawned upon us, we could per-
ceive no vessel of any kind within our horizon. We
had abstracted a compass from the ship, and by its aid,
we readily continued our course to land. About night-
fall, we arrived at the bar of Crofton, and landed at
one of the neglected wharfs. We reported ourselves as
fishermen upon an excursion, and by bribery, procured
what assistance we needed from those who dwelt in those
miserable huts. A suitable coffin and shroud were procured for my father, and it now devolved upon me to
convey his corpse to his residence.

"A steamer was about to ascend the river near
whose banks my father's residence was located. I
applied for tickets, and all the preparations were soon
made. In two days, Pierre and myself landed our cargo. Procuring a suitable vehicle, we soon arrived at
the home of my infancy. An absence of twenty years
had made a great alteration in the appearance of the
old homestead; but time had wrought a still greater

change in me. I learned from one of the servants, who did not recognize me, that my brothers had long since died; but my mother—who was an invalid from grief and from the disappearance of her favorite child a great many years before—rarely ever received visitors.

"My heart was almost broken. I could scarcely summon up sufficient courage to seek my mother's chamber and make the revelation. But should I dread to hasten to the only being who had ever truly loved me? I enquired for the room in which my mother dwelt, and, pushing aside the servant that vainly strove to detain me, I rushed into the presence of her who bore me. When I succeeded in making myself known to her, the joy she manifested was not of this earth.

"We buried my father beside my brothers. My mother expired at the grave, and her lovely form soon reposed beneath the sod of the family cemetery.

"I did not tell you that there were two younger children which had been born during my absence. I left the farm and servants to their care—promising to come again in a few months—but I have never returned. I was so entirely unfitted to associate with respectable men, that I vowed to commence the business of robbery when I should meet with an opportunity. I spent a few months in Crofton, when chance threw me into your society. We formed the band which I headed for so many years, until I resigned my office in favor of Royston.

"You are too familiar with our exploits in this country for me to give you a description of any of them, having been engaged in several of them yourself. But, Hans, you are more expert in planning than in executing, for if there is any danger at hand you are never the foremost.

"It is late ; let us retire to our beds, for I have much upon my mind which I wish to relate to you on the morrow."

Thus ended the tale of Ben Harley. The friends were soon in their beds, and sleep—Heavenly visitor—drowned even the sorrows of those vile men.

8

CHAPTER XII.

" I swear to do this though a present death had been more merciful.
Come on, poor babe ; some powerful spirit instruct the kites and ravens
to be thy nurses ' Wolves and bears, they say, casting their savageness
aside, have done like offices of pity."

Winter's Tale.

It is not necessary to enter into any minute description of the lawless deeds that were enacted at intervals,
at and in the vicinity of Hermit's retreat.   Suffice it to
say, they were generally of a most diabolical character.
From the narrative of Ben Harley, the reader may at
once infer that the wayfaring man, whom chance threw
in their way, was not likely to leave the retreat or its
environs with whole bones and a full purse.

Hans received several valuables from the band before
he left the retreat.   He paid the friends only half of
the intrinsic value of the articles, declaring that, as he
ran a great risk in offering the wares for sale, it was
nothing but right for him to make a good profit.

Leaving Hans to pursue his journey, in whatever
direction he might select for the perfection of his nefa-
rious schemes, the attention of the reader is directed to
other scenes, which may be as interesting as the record
of any of the noted actions of the inimitable Hans
Kremple.

But it may not be out of place to borrow a familiar

figure from one whose name is as familiar in both hem-
ispheres as "household words." **Not Charles Dickens'**
"HOUSEHOLD WORDS," kind reader, for though we consider him a genius, and one of the princes of English
literature, the writer of these pages had rather be excused from quoting from an author who came among us
to enjoy our hospitality, and then, like a frozen adder
warmed into life by kindness, to turn and inflict upon
us a mortal wound.

George Payne Rainesford James, thou incomparable
light novelist, we invoke thy aid. Thou wert surely
born a cavalier, or the "solitary horseman" had never
entered into all thy plots.

It was in the leafy month of June—that happy season of the year, when Southern climes have first made
glad the joyous heart of man. When tree, and shrub,
and vine, are laden with the tender, though delicious
fruits of early summer. It was the hour just before
the king of day hid his blazing head behind the western
hills. The day had nearly closed upon the sins of mortals ; yet the lengthening shadows of the whispering
pines gave but few tokens of approaching night. The
scarce audible tinkle of the distant sheep bell, and the
lowing of the home-returning herds recalled the enthusiast from his rustic dreams, and bade him remember
that he was remote from the noise and clamor of the
busy city.

It was at such an hour that a "solitary horseman"
might have been seen at the distance of more than a
mile from the Hermit's retreat. His noble charger—

whether of the Arabian or Canadian breed, the chronicle doth not relate—had the appearance of having been ridden hard, though his proud spirit could not submit to the goadings of the rowel.

"So ho! Dapple—softly Dapple," said the rider, as he reigned in the horse, "dost not know thy master? By my Halidon, an I had a few more leagues to travel, thou shouldst rue thy conduct."

A powerful mastiff bounded to the stirrup of his master, and signified his joy at the subjection of the horse.

"Down, Wimple, down! dost thou not remember the trouble thou gavest me last night at the inn? Gramercy, sir, an thou troublest me again, thy shaggy skin shall feel the vengeful weight of this whip."

Suiting the action to the words, the powerful rider flecked the sagacious animal more than once, which sent him howling to his proper station in the rear.

The rider was not dressed in "Lincoln Green," nor in the garb of the knights errant, though Brian de Bois Gilbert might have coveted the fine limbs of the unknown. He did not ride with the majestic mien of the "Black Knight," nor with the ease and grace of Wilford of Ivanhoe; yet, there was something very attractive and romantic about his appearance. He was dressed after the fashoin of a gay Southern gentleman, whose chief pleasure is the chase. His dark hair corresponded to the waving black plume that played with his flowing ringlets. His features were concealed by a waxen mask, which gave him rather a cavalier-like appearance.

Reining in his charger with all the grace and digni-

ty of one who was accustomed to the management of
horses, the rider dismounted beside the banks of a soft
rippling brook, and taking his pistols from the holster.
examined the flints and priming, which he found to
be in perfect order. Replacing the pistols with a
self-satisfied air, the "solitary horseman" drew out a
traveling flask, which was filled with delicious spirits,
if an eye-witness could have judged by the pleasure
with which he exhausted a large portion of its contents.
He poured a few drops of the liquid into the nostrils of
the panting horse. This being done, he produced a cup
from his traveling sack, and dipping up water from the
brook, sprinkled it over the head and neck of the horse.

After remaining at the brook a few minutes longer.
the unknown again mounted; and, giving the reins to
Dapple, he was soon speeding swiftly in the direction
of the Hermit's retreat. Wimple had forgotten his late
castigation, and followed the fleet footsteps of Dapple, with much love for his master. The owl hooted
from the hollow oak, the hare fled to the covert, the
shimmering rays of twilight closed up the day, but still
the hardy and dauntless rider kept on his course. (We
thank you, Mr. James, for a few random thoughts.)
By the permission of the reader, we will imagine ourselves (that is, the reader and ego) arrived at the Hermit's retreat a few minutes in advance of the unknown.

Ben Harley and his gang had just returned from the
cave, whither they had been to secure the spoils of the
last expedition. Dandie and dame Elspeth were busily
preparing the repast. The candles were lit in the re-

ception room of the hotel, and the members of the household were waiting patiently for the supper bell to ring.

"Pierre," said Ben, "our last expedition was a bloodless victory, yet we returned home laden with spoils. If there were not so much uncertainty and danger connected with our business, the life we lead here would be a pleasant one, compared to the seafaring existence of a sailor."

"True, Ben," said Pierre, "but then we are put to so much inconvenience in concealing our booty; and then we have to use all sorts of expedients to keep from detection. Just remember, only a few days since, you and I were so hotly pursued by the officers that we barely had time to spring into the copse, and hastily transform ourselves into ragged mendicants—which we did with so much adroitness that we were not suspected by the beagles of justice, as they passed in full pursuit of—*ourselves.*"

"I suspect, Pierre, that you long again to be in a condition to shed blood more freely than we do here. You soulless heathen! Is it not sufficient that you take the last *sous* from the trembling traveler? Yet, we can scarcely withhold you from slaying every one we despoil of his purse and other valuables. Ah! Pierre, you will have to render a strange account to your Maker one of these days."

"Softly, Ben," said Pierre, as he laughingly directed a knowing glance to the window where Ben sat, "you speak as lightly as if you had never aimed a deadly stroke of the cincter at the head of that fat Dutchman who was imploring you to save his life."

" Quiet, Pierre," retorted Ben, " I was not much to blame ; you know I could never make head or tail out of that delightful language. How did I know what the thick tongued foreigner was saying ? "

" But, Ben, the signal of distress is always legible, it mattereth not what signs are made to represent it."

" Oh ! you piratical imp," said Ben, " to listen at your jargon, one would be disposed to think that you had turned preacher and abjured the wickedness of your ways."

" Ben," said Pierre, " let us be quits on those scores. When have you heard from Carl ? "

" I do not know," replied Ben, " It seems——"

Here the sentence of the outlaw was cut short by the sound of horses' feet near at hand.

" What can the fellow mean ?" said Ben, as the shrill notes of a bugle saluted their ears. " The man must be a herald of an Eastern troop just from Palestine. I do wonder if the wand of Merlin has transported us to another hemisphere, and the wheels of Time have rolled back five centuries ? These are strange times. Pierre ; go and see what sir Knight wanteth."

Pierre went as he was directed, and perceiving that the unknown was masked and spoke not, his knees shook under him. He supposed that he stood in the presence of a spectre horseman, or the shades of one of those luckless men whom his bloody hands had sent to his last account. Running back to Ben, Pierre declar-

ed that the place was haunted or was about to be put
under a "spell." Pierre ran to the sofa and hid his
head between its cushioned pillows, while Ben went, himself, to ask the rider in what manner he could be served.

Approaching the horseman, Ben made a very polite
bow, and asked in genteel phrase after the health of the
unknown knight. (We must imitate G. Payne Rainesford once more.) "Polite sir," replied the unknown,
"I am on a pilgrimage to the shrine of my lady of the
BROKEN HEART. She resideth only a days' journey
from this spot, as my directions, given me by the 'Sisters of Mercy' at my departure from my castle, plainly
indicate. It behooveth me to pay adorations at her
sainted shrine, and I have a burden at my heart which
cannot be removed except by her forgiveness. I crave
rest for myself and refreshments for my horse and dog,
(may Saint Barnabas protect them!) but as for me, no
food except that which hath been sanctified by the prayers of the "Sisters of Mercy" must enter these lips
until I shall have knelt me at the shrine of my lady of
the BROKEN HEART."

" Alight, sir knight," said Ben, who was determined
to explore this mystery. "Our cottage shall be your
resting place for one night. No pilgrim to the shrine
of my lady of the BROKEN HEART shall ever be turned
from our door. Here, Pedro, see to the horse; and
you, sir pilgrim, follow me, and I will conduct you into
our humble castle. Ho! warden, lower the port cullis
and admit your commandant and his guest." But,
awaking from the enchantment which the pious words

of the unknown had thrown around him, the infatuated
Ben implored the forgiveness of his stately companion,
who, approaching the unsanctified person of the fierce
robber, whisperad a few words into his ear, which produced a perceptible change in the demeanor of Ben.

"Your instructions shall be obeyed to the letter; and
we must keep up the deceptive appearance," said Ben,
who conducted him into the reception room.

Dame Elspeth commenced counting her beads, as she
dropped a plate of savory victuals in the yard. She
was certain her time had come. She imagined that the
arch-fiend had come to claim and bear her off as a prize.

"May the saints beshrew me," said Dandie, as he
hastened to the relief of his spouse, "the wife is daft,
yet blessings upon her, she hath a braver heart than
mine. What cowards doth conscience make of us all!"

"Pull off your visor, sir knight," said Ben as he led
the unknown to a seat, "and taste some of our refreshments."

"It is not permitted me by my vow," replied the unknown, "to discover my features to mortal until I have
paid my vows at the shrine of my lady of the BROKEN
HEART."

"'Tis he, 'tis he," said Pierre, "'tis my victim," as
he rushed from the room, followed by his companions,
leaving the unknown and Ben alone. The former was
shown to his room, while the latter in vain endeavored
to collect his friends around the festive board. It is
needless to add, that the room of the unknown was not
entered that night for the purpose of robbery, nor were

Dapple and Wimple disturbed. By early dawn, Ben brought out the horse, and the unknown vaulted into the saddle. "You may rely upon me," said Ben, "I will be there with assistance." They parted, and the horseman was soon out of sight.

When Ben summoned Pierre and his comrades, he could scarcely make them leave their rooms. In order that he might keep up the appearance of mystery, he told them that no stranger had been there, but supposed they must have been disturbed by ugly dreams.

By the leave of the reader, the scene changes from Hermit's retreat to the house of Mr. Rockford. On the evening of the day subsequent to the departure of the " unknown knight " from the Hermit's retreat, Mr. Rockford was sitting in his piazza, reading to his wife, while Sebastian, whom we have not seen in several months, was playing upon the front yard with his pets.

" Josephine," said the husband, " Sebastian has grown so much lately that Captain Walsingham will scarcely recognize him when he comes to see us to-morrow. The boy looks so handsome in the new suit you have made him, suppose we let the nurse take him down to the beach and play a while in the shade. He loves to see the waves lash upon the shore."

The request of the father was complied with, and Sebastian kissed his parents and departed with the nurse. Mr. Rockford continued his reading until it was time for him to go to his office. On his way thither he met Hans Kremple, going towards the sea-side, in company with a stranger who appeared to be lame, having the appearance of a foreigner. A huge pair of green spectacles gave the stranger a comical expression.

"Hans has more strange acquaintances than any man in Crofton," said Mr. Rockford to himself, as he hurried past them. Before he arrived at the office, Mr. Rockford encountered Mr. Snibbens, who had just dismissed his school. The pedagogue bored the good man to the *quick* in trying to illustrate something beyond his own comprehension.

Mr. Rockford was busily engaged in the investigation of a "case," and was hunting up all the "points," when one of his servants, hastily entering his office. implored him to return home immediately, as something dreadful had happened. Mr. Rockford was a man not easily excited, but was generally disposed to encounter and overcome obstacles with composure. Supposing that his presence at his own house was absolutely necessary, he hastened home, much troubled in mind.

When he entered his house, he found everything in utter confusion. The servants were running in every direction. Mrs. Rockford ran about the house almost frantic. Mr. Rockford was horror-stricken when he learned that Sebastian had been taken from the nurse by a party of men who had landed in haste from a boat, and. before she could give the alarm, they had pushed from shore and sailed away.

CHAPTER XIII.

THE reader must now imagine that five years have passed away since the strange abduction of Sebastian Rockford. We must now change the scene of our story from Crofton, and introduce new characters into our romance, and follow up, if possible, the fortunes of our little hero.

The greatest men who have ever figured upon the stage of life, and whose actions have been noted, either descended from the Plebian race, or their road to fame was traversed with dangers and difficulties. It is a singular fact, and one worthy of note, that men may be born to wealth, but individuals must work their way to distinction. Alfred the Great, who was one of the most valiant kings that ever sat upon the throne of the British nation, was an outcast and a beggar in his own country, until the Fates decreed that a wise man should be called back to the helm of State.

Wise men, on the contrary, have declared that our fortunes are not in our stars, but in ourselves. If such be the fact, then the science of Astrology is at an end. Two thousand years have passed since the wise Chaldeans looked up at the Heavenly bodies and read the future history of nations by the fitful changes of the twinkling stars. Antiquity itself has taken its rise since prophecies have ceased to be promulgated by peripatetic philosophers, or by those wise and good men whose solitary yet holy tread have worn away the flag-stones of deep dungeons.

Who that is an enthusiast and an admirer of the Heavenly bodies, has not watched the motions of the planets and wished that a sign might be given unto him? You are a coward, and it can be very plainly demonstrated even to your own satisfaction. You start at an apparition in a dream, and the cold sweat bedews your brow, and you thrust your timid head under the bed clothes on awaking, for fear that you, in reality, may behold the realization of your "poetic nightmare." Dare you at such times walk into a cemetery and commune alone with the spirits of departed friends? You shrink from the task; you fear that you might call up spirits from the vasty deep which would not down at your bidding. They are not morally brave who start at the apparitions of night. Those that sleep the sleep of death are our best friends, or we should be infested with numberless foes. The very dust you tread upon was once a component part of a human being, and dare you fear the soil you may call your own?

Oh! reader, if the dead are permitted to walk forth at night, they will be seen only in your feverish imagination, or in your dreams.

Do you love fiction? listen at the conversation of the giddy crowds that throng your thoroughfares. If they have lately come into possession of a fact, the rules of addition and subtraction will soon make truth appear stranger than fiction.

Truth dwells at the bottom of a well. Would you imbibe a draught? take a glass of pure water, and cool your feverish imagination. Do not expect to find a gold mine in every furrow you open, nor expect a marvelous revelation in every page of legitimate lore you peruse. The authors of the Arabian Nights, Don Quixotte and Gil Blas, exhausted the fund of thrilling adventure, and we can never supplant or rival them.

When Moses was placed in the ark, which preserved his life, did it occur to his mother that she was rescuing from destruction the future patriarch and leader of the children of God? Oh! skeptical reader, believe not that all things happen by chance.

If we deal in a few reflections now and then, have not Fielding, Scott and Bulwer done the same? We ought at least to be allowed as much license as some of our funny female writers, (God bless and put them all to some occupation that is more remunerative than writing for one dollar and fifty-cents a column!) who spin out sixteen pages a day in descanting upon the travels of a certain toady in Lapland. One of those blessed ladies, who has swept all Southern male authors from the gay pages of Romance with one shake of her curls, once wrapped herself up in a buffalo robe with— we shall not call *its* name—at any rate, this was only in imagination. She had read the book of travels, and having nothing else to write about, she got into the sleigh with *it*, (remember, reader, this was only in fancy) and traveled all over Lapland, Russia and Norway with Baron Toady, all in sixteen pages of manuscript! Bless the dear creature ! she is perfectly sincere when she declares that men have but little genius. We had rather be wanting in genius than to strive to imitate every toadyish tale writer and poetaster who have forgotten how to call things by their proper names.

We have no distaste to the writings of the ladies, but we would have beautiful governments if their wise (?) mandates were followed up. There are only two lady authors whose works can stand the test of criticism— we mean as distinguished writers—and those are Jane Porter and Madame De Stael. Their mission seemed to be to wreath garlands of immortality of ivy green to crown their noble heads.

We have a few man-milliners in the United States, who surely belong to the class of MISTAKENDOM.— Let them commence writing upon whatever subject they please, they will make it convenient to quarrel with the fashionable ladies of "Madison Square" about the flounces of their dresses, the feathers upon the edges of their fans; and some of them have wisely invented rouges and pomades, and a thousand little things for the ladies that *they* (the ladies) never thought of themselves. Those man-milliners are so delicately modest that, instead of calling a silver thimble by its proper name, they will denominate it a semi-perforated argental truncated cone. Others, though bachelors, would not dare to undress in a room in which there is a pin-cushion, because the needles have eyes. Those fashionable critics have given rise to the Flora McFlimseys who, though "arrayed in purple," havn't a thing in the wide world to wear.

Dear, gentle reader, if we were able we would not
distort your imagination by relating hair breadth es-
capes and impossible improbabilities. We have seen a
few things which we durst not relate, for fear of being
considered a fabricator. We once knew a man who was
so fond of the marvelous, that Truth, to him, dwelt so
deep in the well, that his bucket never reached the retreat of the nymph.

We commenced this chapter by notifying the indulgent reader that five years have passed since the abduction of our little hero.

Yonder is a beautiful, though an unostentatious mansion. Theodore Manning is the possessor of a thousand
acres of arable land. His many servants till his pro-
ductive fields, and the products of their labor yield him
an ample support.

Two little boys were playing in the shady yard in
front of the house. One of them was only four years
of age, and the other was about seven. If the former
had nothing remarkable about him, the latter could not
have been passed carelessly by. His soft blue eyes and
auburn hair were so remarkable that his childish beauty
made you glad. The boys were arranging their toys,
when Mr. Manning came out to join in the sport.

"Come here, Falkner," said Mr. Manning, speaking to the elder, "here are some new marbles for you
—divide them with Corolan."

"I thank you, my father," said the boy, "let me kiss
you for them."

"Bless the boy!" murmured the farmer, "he is the
very light of my home."

"See, Corolan," said Falkner, "see the pretty marbles papa has brought us—here are yours."

"Give me all of 'em here," said Corolan, "you always take the biggest and the prettiest." And the child —after making his own selections, and claiming the largest share—asked his father what else he had for him.

"Don't you thank papa for them. brother?" said Falkner.

"I don't know," said the boy, "he brings us things because he wants to."

"You are rather an ungrateful boy, Corie," said his father, "I have brought Falkner another book," and he drew out a pictorial reader, which he gave him. The boy kissed him again, and read several passages to his father.

"It is time you were off to school, Falkner—your teacher says you must not be late. The boy hastened to the school, while Mr. Manning played with Corolan. He was not able to interest Corolan, and, calling to his mother, the boy was delivered to her. Corolan dearly loved his mother—who returned his love with compound interest. She was kind to Falkner, too, but her affections were doubly centered upon the younger.

If there was any difference exhibited by the mother in the management of the children, it had no external appearance. She had too pure a heart to be so far influenced by caprice as to mistreat one of the children; yet, it must be confessed that Corolan was her favorite. If the mother centered her affections upon the one, the father had a secret love for the other that showed itself too plainly, at times, to be entirely concealed.

"Wife," said the father, "are you carefully preserving those relics that were found with the child, and the letter which was concealed in the wrapper? We may be compelled to have recourse to them some of these days."

"They are kept in a trunk to themselves," said the wife, "and the key is never allowed to pass into the hands of a third person."

"I am often forced to the point of belief that the child was taken from a highly respectable family by violence. It seems as if we were doing a wrong deed to keep the secret; yet, the letter was couched in such ambiguous language that a publication in a paper would endanger the life of Falkner. We must be contented to abide our time."

"I am perfectly contented," replied the wife, "to rest the whole matter in your hands."

Those faithful parents could not consent to make the revelation to a living soul; and Falkner was supposed by many to be their own son. It is true, he had, but little resemblance to Corolan, but the affection the parents exhibited for him was the best evidence of his being their child.

CHAPTER XIV.

FALKNER MANNING was a very promising boy at seven years of age ; and when he had completed his ninth year, he had made so rapid a progress in his primary studies, it was evident that he could easily enter upon a higher course. He received the joyful tidings one moring, from his father—who placed a Latin Grammar in his hands —that he might commence the study of that useful language. He had but little difficulty in acquiring a correct pronunciation from the wholesome iustructions of his competent teacher, whose plan was not different from the masters of the old school. He insisted that one book thoroughly learned, was of incalculably greater advantage to a boy than a confused knowledge of a dozen folios.

Falkner was continued upon the Grammar until he was enabled to analyze every portion of it readily. The instructor had satisfied himself that there was no railroad to learning. The mind is so constituted, reasoned he, that it cannot be forced. By constant application, and frequent repetition, a thorough knowledge of the primary rules of the most intricate language may be learned by a boy of ordinary abilities ; but it takes the study of long years to attain to any degree of perfec-

tion in a language so difficult as that of the ancient
Romans.   Falkner read the primers and Julius Cæsar's
Commentaries upon the Gallic War, in two years from
the time of his entry upon the study of the language.
At the examination he received a silver medal from the
board of examiners, for proficiency in Latin composition.   Mr. Manning pressed him to his bosom when
they arrived at home, while Mrs. Manning participated
in the enjoyment.   As a reward for his industry, a fine
suit of green cloth, trimmed with braid, adorned the
beautiful form of the fair-haired boy.   Corolan was
made the recipient of one from the same piece; though
his idle habits had sent him to the foot of the class.
He declared that he would not learn, and he wished
every day was Saturday, in order that he might hunt,
and fish, and ride his pony.

"Now, Corie," said Falkner, "father is so anxious
for you to be a good scholar, do put up those useless
toys and that noisy whip, and come to the table and let
me teach you how to find your map questions."

"I do not care if he does, Master Falkner—as the
teacher calls you.   Father need not send me to the hate-
ful old school unless he wants to; besides, I despise the
old rivers and towns with hard names.   If you bring
that dirty old map to me again to-night, I'll dash it in
the fire."   Here Falkner left him to his amusements.

Corolan was as petulant and quarrelsome as Falkner
was kind and submissive.   The former was governed by
coercion and presents—the latter by duty.   He could
never be induced to disregard the injunctions of his pa-

rents, or the rules of the school of which he was the brightest ornament.

Vacation had come, with all its golden prospects of fishing, hunting, gathering fruit, and excursions upon horse-back. Corolan, instead of imitating the laudable example of Falkner, in the preparation of his lessons for the examination, which had lately passed off so much to the credit of the latter, had neglected his books for the purpose of arranging his fishing tackle and other implements of sport.

"Come, my sons," said the father a few days after vacation had commenced, put on your hunting suits and let us go to the low grounds and shoot birds. You are not old enough yet, Corie, to learn the art of shooting. When you shall have grown larger, Falkner will give you the necessary instructions."

"Papa," said Corolan, pouting and about to get into one of his ugly fits, "I had rather not go, if Falkner is allowed to take a gun. He learned to shoot during last vacation ; yet, I have never fired a gun unless you were holding it."

"Come, darling," said his mother, who had been listening to the conversation, "go on with father and brother Falkner, and when you return I will give you some nice cakes."

The boy was humbled into submission by the entreaties of his mother. He kissed her, and drying his tears, made instant preparations for the excursion.— Falkner endeavored to assist him in dressing, but he put aside the hand of the good boy, and bade him attend to

his own affairs—saying if he was not big enough to
shoot, he had sense enough to arrange his own dress.
He would gladly imitate the actions of Falkner, but if
the latter ever made. any suggestions, the stubborn
Corie would change his plans.

The dogs were unkennelled and brought out. The
sagacious animals were so glad of an opportunity of
exercising their limbs, that they bounded over the head
of Corie, who took them, and started in full speed to the
field. The father directed Falkner to follow, and detain them at the spring branch until he arrived; or the
birds would be flushed before he was prepared to shoot
them. The boy did as he was directed. When he came
up to where Falkner was holding on to the dogs, he observed that Corie was vexed with his brother. Mr.
Manning took out his whip and gave the pointers a short
exercise in *gravitation*. As the *falling* strokes lit upon
their shaggy sides, they were brought to their senses.
Corie was threatened with his displeasure if he did not
act like a pretty little boy.

They entered a grove, shaded by tall oak and hickory
trees, which beautify the Southern forests. The birds
played among the branches, and called one another with
plaintive notes. The mocking-bird echoed all their mel-
odies in sweeter strains than the original. Nature has
given that songster powers of imitation unequalled by
man himself; yet the natural note of the melodious bird
is but a harsh, discordant sound. Ventriloquists, jest
ers and imitators are gifted in this respect by nature,
for the absence of brains. If a man will not attempt

to sound his own trump, he **must** sound the trump of others.

"Bear in mind, Falkner, that we are to admire the songs of the mocking-bird, but we have a purpose, or an aim in life to strive after. We must cut ourselves loose from leading-strings and fashion out our own course. If that stream yonder remained still, and re-solved itself into a turbid lake, the waters would be un-healthy, and the country would be filled with miasma. But, look how swiftly the current glides on. The stream is constantly receiving new springlets. Yonder is a small branch winding around the bend, to augment its waters. See that cascade, where we delight to bathe, near the place where I taught you to swim. That small river widens and deepens in its course, as it winds majestically through the forests, and thousands are glad-dened by its refreshing influence. One hundred miles below here it empties into the ocean. That world of waters is formed by the numberless streams like this. Were it not for them, do you suppose the ocean would exist? That stream, my boy, is the type of human life. Man, if he allows himself to become a sluggard, is like the sluggish pool, but the active, smart, indus-trious worker, if he accumulates property, whether for himself or not, is like the beautiful river that we are just approaching."

"True, father," replied the thoughtful boy, "that is why I admire the works of Cæsar. He had but little time to spare from his duties as a general."

"You remember, Falkner, that when the army of Cæ-

sar was not upon the march, or in actual engagements
on the field of battle, it was in winter quarters. It
was in the camp that he composed his Commentaries."

"How could he find so much time even there to write,
father? I am sure he had much to do in constructing
fortifications for defence."

"Falkner," replied the father, much interested in the
conversation, "Cæsar had many lieutenants, or subal-
terns whom he commanded to have particular care in
seeing to the drilling of the men. He may not have
appeared upon parade more than once a month."

"I remember," said Falkner, "something about for-
tifying the camps, and leading the soldiers from the
winter quarters. '*Cæsar castella Galliae muniverat et
tres legiones ex hibernis eduxerat.*'"

Here the conversation was broken off by Corolan,
who, having espied a covey of partridges under the
copse, hastened to his father and reported the fact.
Falkner was requested to stand prepared to shoot as
soon as his father gave the word. The well trained dogs
were quickly upon the scent, and at the signal from Mr.
Manning, the birds were flushed. When they rose,
three were shot down by Mr. Manning, who commanded
Falkner to discharge his piece. The boy shot either
too soon or too late, as he missed entirely."

"I think I could beat that shooting myself, master
Falkner," said Corie—who seemed to be glad at the ill
success of his brother.

"I hope you can, Corie," said the good brother. "I
am not at all averse to your being enabled to excell in
some things."

In a few minutes Falkner had an opportunity of testing his marksmanship again when he was more successful—having brought down two birds. When the father and sons had bagged as many birds as they cared to carry home, they sought the cool shade on the banks of the stream.

"Now, Corie," said the father, "you are fond of sporting with the hook and line; suppose you rig up some of those reed staffs that lie yonder, and let us have some sport to divert you."

"I have the hooks and lines," replied the boy, "but where shall we get worms from?"

"They are easily supplied, my boy; bend down one of those green boughs over your head, and supply yourself with Catawba worms."

"Those green monsters! they look too frightful, sir, I had rather not touch them," said the boy.

"They are perfectly harmless," said the mild, but intrepid Falkner, as he pulled them from their leafy homes and handed them to his father.

"There are but few things," said the good man to his interesting sons, "which the Almighty has formed for our use that are not harmless. The venomous reptiles that attack us unawares are not only poisonous, but deadly to the taste. God has pointed out to us as if by instinct, what fruits, herbs and animals we should use for food. We long to pluck the luscious plum, grape, apple and peach, but we shrink from the touch of a prickly pear, crab-apple or persimmon. Learn to improve those tastes while you are yet young, and you may make *connoiseurs* in the culinary art."

"Have all animals hearts?" said Corolan to his father.

"Certainly, my son ; but why do you ask the question ?"

"Because, I heard you and Falkner repeating the lesson, ' *Omne animal quod sanguinem habet, habet etiam cor.*' I heard you tell brother that the translation was, ' Every animal which has blood, has also a heart.' "

"I think you are improving, master Corolan, in our vacation," said the delighted Falkner, "you are surely sharpening up your wits."

"Not at all, sir, but as I am compelled to listen at the two hours' drilling father gives you every night, I would be very dull if I were not enabled to pick up *some* phrases. When I drop to sleep and commence dreaming about the fish biting or the pony galloping, I am certain to be waked up by yours and father's never-ending *jamsquams* and *quidquids*."

" The boy is no dolt at last," murmured his father, "if he is never to be skilled in books, he may surely turn to be a good politician or 'a broker.

After spending an hour in the pleasant sport of fishing, they wound up their lines, much pleased with having drawn out several fine fish.

When they reached home, laden with fish, birds and fruits, the mother had an elegant luncheon spread for them, in which the cakes and sweet meats for Corie were not forgotten.

CHAPTER XV.

THE happiest days of our lives are those of our childhood; yet, how heedlessly the rising generation reject the sage advice of their elders, who warn them not to spend their time in idleness, but advise them to use every moment as a precious gift from the great ruler of the universe. While one boy voluntarily seeks those silent companions which speak as with a voice from the tomb. one thousand will lay those wise monitors upon the dusty shelves.

Do you wish to be wise and have your names engraved upon the temple of Fame ? then the lark must not find you slumbering upon your downy beds. You must be watchful, and not lose one golden moment. Do not un dertake a greater task than you can perform. Measure your abilities by the proper standard, and if your powers of mind are great, place your mark high ; you may never arrive at eminence by striving for honors of a medium grade. Do you know where to find the key that can unlock more treasures than lie hidden in the mines of California ? it lies concealed in your resolution—it is PERSEVERANCE. Nearly all great men have sprung from obscure families. Can you doubt this ? look to the pages of History. Where the crown or the reins of government have passed into the hands of an heir apparent, and where new republics and empires have arisen upon the ruins of tottering nations, the descendants of the persevering plebian race have always pressed to the front ranks.

Coriolanus, who sprang from the ranks of the Plebians of Rome, assumed the command of her armies with as much pride as any of the representatives of the exalted race of the Scipios. When fallen into disgrace at home, he led the armies of the enemies of his country to the gates of the city with the insatiate revenge of an insulted potentate. The nobles of Rome bowed in humble submission to him; but he withdrew the besieging thousands from the walls of his native city, alone at the entreaties of his revered mother.

The man possessed of true merit, and lofty intellect, coupled with goodness of heart, and integrity of purpose, be he poor, or endowed with the wealth of a prince, should alone be the ruler of a free people. If a tyrant oppresses you, slay him—if kings strive to rule over you, depose them. Never be contented to bow the head of a freeman in the presence of a crowned prince. The days of princes were ended when Christ appeared upon earth. You are as good as a king. To-day he may flourish, but to-morrow his subjects may drag him to the scaffold.

But to proceed with our story. If we digress now and then, we only imitate the example of those who are our superiors in the art of composition. Our readers become tired of the dull monotony of a bare narrative —so do we—hence the digression.

Two boys who have been reared up together as brothers, having received the same kind attentions from indulgent parents, were never more unlike than Falkner and Corolan. If there was nothing vicious and sordid about the latter, he possessed but few or none of the ennobling traits of the former. Falkner was an exception to the majority of boys of his age. If he read a book, it was with care that he tried to profit by its wise instructions. His father had so lectured him upon the first principles of literature, that he was readily enabled to judge of the merits and demerits of any composition. Nature seemed to have formed him for a scholar, and his father intended to give him all the benefits of a liberal education. Corolan should enjoy the same opportunities, too, though he might not profit thereby.

Some of our readers will remember that a promise was made in the commencement of this book, that a variety of scenes should be introduced to please all classes of those who delight in reading romances. If we introduce the wise teacher of those interesting boys, and give a few of his "wise saws and modern instances," will the reader grow tired? We hope not.

"Yonder comes old Heflin now," said Corie to Falkner, as the Manning family lingered at the breakfast table one fine morning during vacation, "I do wonder what the old crow wants now? Come, master Falkner, you and father rub up your Latin; as for me, I see enough of the old owl during school time. Good morning to you all; I'll just ride to the post office and get father's papers."

" What a strange boy you are, Corie," said the father, who was both amused and vexed at the remarks of his son, "if dominie Heflin is an odd old man, he is a fine teacher, and deserves **your** respect."

" That is all true, father, but I shall love him better when I have ceased to be one of his pupils. Falkner, don't you crawl down his throat or let him carry you off in one of those large pockets. If I were father I would send you to live with the old fellow. If you have any occasion to send all your silver and copper pieces to his dirty, tow-headed children, like you have done before, remember that Corie Manning has an equal share in the contents of our trunk."

" You need not be alarmed, brother; I have not the least desire to kneel to our good teacher, or to load him with useless presents. You ought to remember how you implore him to spare you when your laziness puts you at the foot of the class."

The old dominie knocked at the front door; and while Falkner hastened to give him admission, Corie made his escape into his mother's room, thence to the stables. His father smiled as he saw him riding off at a brisk speed in the direction of the post office.

Dominie Heflin was not so erudite as dominie Sampson, but he chose to display more of his learning than that strange genius, who will be remembered as long as Walter Scott's works are read, but he was more fond of talking than Harry Bertram's tutor was. He could never bear to remain silent. He retailed his wisdom at every step he took. It mattered not who was the lis-

tener, dominic Heflin—when once his text was taken—
never left off speaking until the subject was quite exhausted. He was not like the young man who sought
an introduction to Madame de Stael. The extraordinary lady rebuked him, and left him, because he could
not advance one idea, good or bad. If the domine had
lived in her circle, perhaps she might have been amused
with his strange pedantry.

He wore a long, black camlet oversack, which reached nearly to his feet. A pair of tight-fitting pants was
intercepted in their downward progress by stockings.
The old man wore his hair in a cue, and his head was
covered with a quaker-like hât of the olden time. The
Vicar of Wakefield and the dominie would have made a
pair. He was what might justly be termed a locomotive encyclopedia, or a circulating library.

"*Diem bonam tibi opto,* master Falkner, *sol splendide
fulget, hodie,*" said the dominie, as he walked into the
parlor.

"*Gaudeo te valere,*" said the boy, who had learned
some phrases from the master.

"Your humble servant, friend Manning," said the
delighted dominie, as he took his seat to commence a
four hour's chat, "time hangs so heavily upon my hands
at home during vacation, that I become heartily tired
of conversing with the 'gude wife and bairns,' inasmuch
as their ideas and mine run in pretty much the same
channel."

"You are heartily welcome, friend Heflin," said the
good Mr. Manning, "I am quite glad to see you at all

times. It gives me an opportunity of rubbing up my
Latin and Greek to talk with you.   I am never better
employed than when engaged in advancing the interest
of education.   I am not fond of a display of too much
pedantry, but an intellectual debate upon the ancient
classics is never out of place when we can benefit our
children by the conversation.   Corie is not fond of his
books, but Falkner is never better satisfied than when
perusing the work of a classic author.   Do you think
you can prepare Falkner for the Freshman class of
M—— University in two years?"

"By all means," replied the dominie, "he is quite
ready to commence reading Virgil, and by your consent
he shall immediately take up the study of Greek.   Boys
are never prepared to commence the latter language until they have mastered the rudiments of the Latin.   It
is altogether a mistake, sir, to force a lad through the
course.   They may be enabled, by constant application, to
memorize all the rules of those languages in a short space
of time, but whether they can retain what they so hastily
learn, is another thing.   As I have told you before,
'Squire, the mind cannot be forced.   It must imbibe
right reason by degrees.   One chapter, or one book
well digested, is worth more to a boy than the incom-
plete understanding of the works of a dozen authors.
Let us prove it: we can only relate what we have
learned thoroughly, and make it intelligible to our hearers.   If the mind is burdened with a thousand different
things, the reasoning faculties will become obtuse."

"You are correct, dominie," said Mr. Manning, "a few

lessons well learned each day, will soon make up the fund of a boy's education."

"True, my friend," said the dominie, "that is exactly what I endeavor to teach my lads, *non quam multum, sed quam bene.* There is another wise saying, which is worth its weight in gold, *labor omnia vincit.* If I can not teach a boy to observe all these wise sayings, and conform entirely to my precepts, I almost despair of his ever arriving at proficiency. I exhaust every possible plan before I confess that I can not teach a boy who has even common capacity. Some of the best and most accurate scholars we read of, either in ancient or modern times, were very dull boys. But patience and perseverence on the part of their instructors, overcame every obstruction. You must not be too uneasy about the backwardness of Corolan. He has an excellent mind, but his ideas have not yet been reached. He is averse to study. If he ever learns much, it must be either voluntarily or from observation."

The dominie made use of many Latin, Greek and French quotations during the conversation, which we omit from the fact that many of our readers are not linguists. Falkner was an atttentive listener and often joined in the conversation. Mr. Manning knew that the dominie was versed in English as well as Latin poetry. In order to draw him out on some other subject, he changed the conversation.

"What are your ideas of happiness, dominie Heflin?" said the host.

10

"It exists as much in our imagination as in anything else, I think," replied the teacher.

"Suppose we should imagine ourselves miserable?"

"Then, my friend, there is an end to the enigma; for you may safely say that happiness is a riddle too." (*Aquam da mihi,* master Falkner.)

While the youth ordered a glass of water, the father brought out the wine. At the sight of the cut glass decanters and silver goblets, the eyes of the dominie sparkled, and he almost forgot his enunciation of happiness.

"*Rogo te aquam, sed mihi vinum das,*" and the dominie drank the health of his friend in more than one glass. The domine was upon the point of feeling a portion of what some men call happiness, and he thus commenced:

"You ask my opinion in regard to happiness. I will just quote a few lines from the bard of Twickenham:

> ' Oh, Happiness! our being's end and aim,
> Good, pleasure, ease, content' whate'er thy name:
> That something still which prompts the eternal sigh,
> For which we bear to live, or dare to die:
> Which still so near us, yet beyond us lies,
> O'erlooked, seen double, by the fool and wise:
> Plant of celestial seed! if dropped below,
> Say in what mortal soil thou deign'st to grow?'

Here we have what happiness is, and what it may not be. We cannot deny that all men desire to exist in a state of bliss, yet their mode of living may differ as widely as the habits of the animals of the Torrid and North Frigid Zones. The pleasure of this man may consist in drinking and riotous living, while the enjoyment of another may be exactly the reverse. One man may love ease—another is not contented unless he is in continual motion. We may have happiness within our grasp, yet sigh for enjoyments which may lead to misery. Thus, you see, happiness is a myth, or a will-o-the-wisp. It may be ever in sight, yet, like the mirage of the desert, vanish into air as we approach it.''

"But, dominie," said the host, "are you not sure that Pope was right in his deductions, or do you not think he was melancholy at times, and longed for things he did not need?''

"It is hard to tell," said the patriarch of Academus, "we must take a man's writings at what they are worth. He has but few equals as an essayist, and no superiors as an original thinker and correct versifier.''

"Alexander Pope," rejoined Mr. Manning, "had correct views upon any subject. If he had lived in our day, when learning has received so many auxiliaries, he would have left us a greater legacy than he has. But let us look and see what he says further upon our subject in point:

> Order is Heaven's first law ; and this confessed,
> Some are, and must be, greater than the rest,
> More rich, more wise ; but who infers from hence
> That such are happier, shocks all common sense.'

"Here, my good Heflin, we are assured that happiness is not alone confined to the wealthy classes. It is very natural for us to hear some men long for wealth, while others, who are rich in heaps of gold, long for the repose that is bought only by a competency. For the very reason that we are never satisfied, we may rightly infer that happiness is only a relative term.— When a limit shall have been placed to our desires, then we may know how to appreciate happiness. I fear, sometimes, it is like a humming-bird. It is almost a miracle to catch one, and when you confine the little Peri, it dies. To sum up the whole subject and place it in a nut-shell, Happiness is LIBERTY."

The dominie was about to enter at large upon several points, but the dinner-bell was heard, and the discussion ended.

The meal was scarcely concluded, when one of the servants entered the room hastily and told the master that the black pony had come back without Corolan. There was much confusion in the house for the next few minutes. When Mrs. Manning had been sufficiently quieted, her husband followed the dominie and Falkner, who had taken some of the servants and gone in quest of the missing boy.

CHAPTER XVI.

WHEN we least expect danger it is at our door.—
Though we may linger in the paths of pleasure and
gather flowers from all the hedges, yet a serpent may
lie hidden in the rosy bower to inflict upon us the mortal wound.   Is it better for us to long for all the pleasures of earth at once, and to expect the full train of evils
to flood in upon us in their natural course afterwards,
or to long for an alternation of the good and the evil?
It is difficult for us to bring our minds to a right deci-
sion.

All things do not happen by chance, or the whole
fabric of the Christian religion would be overthrown.
It was necessary in olden times for prophecies to be
fulfilled, which gave some semblance to FATALISM; yet.
both Moral law and the light of reason dispell that in-
fatuation.   If God moves in a mysterious way, it is not
for us to divine the cause, or demand the reason.
There are thousands of things—as we are taught—
which will not be revealed to us until the day of JUDG-
MENT.   Why cannot man discern all things?   Why is
it not given him to explore all the foundations of science?
Was he not forbidden to eat of the fruit of the Tree of
Life?   Let us reason a while.   Why can not a man pull

down a house from its firm foundations? Simply for
the reason that he is not an elephant. Why can he not
survey the starry Heavens and discover new planets
without the aid of a telescope? Simply because the
Great I AM hath placed those bodies too far for his
vision to scan.

> " Why has not man a microscopic eye ?
> For this plain reason : man is not a fly."

If the father of Corolan had known what evil would
have befallen his son, his influence and fatherly kindness would have kept the boy a close prisoner at home.
But Mr. Manning was like the majority of men; he
was perfectly willing to trust to chance in some respect.
The paths that youth are compelled to tread are so be-
sprinkled with flowers and thorns, that every step is a
venture. But to our narrative.

Corolan saddled the black pony, and having mounted.
rode off briskly in the direction of Oak-Lawn—the village at which his father recieved his mails. As we have
before related, the boy had a will of his own. He was
possessed of a dauntless spirit, and if he took it into
his head to accomplish an object, he would never desist
from an endeavor until he had tried every expedient.
If he had possessed the same aptitude for his studies
that he did for sport and pleasure, Falkner would never
have supplanted him in the estimation of the dominie.

The principal object that Corie had in view on that
morning, was to rid himself of the presence of his
teacher, for whom he entertained no good will. He

urged the pony into a canter—the submissive quadruped obeyed. He pressed him to the utmost extent of his speed—still the pony made no resistance. For two miles the caprices of the boy vexed and tortured the pony from the most tardy to the swiftest gait.

When Corolan had spent as much time at the office as he desired, in playing marbles and ball with his acquaintances, he applied for and received his father's mail, and started towards home. When he had accomplished about one-half of the distance between the office and his father's house, he endeavored to urge the panting pony into a full speed; but the reluctant beast—tired out with cruel treatment from his young master—became restive and threw him upon the roadside.

When dominie Heflin and Falkner approached the spot where the unconscious boy lay, they were rejoiced to discover that he was not dead. Mr. Manning arrived soon with the family physician, whom he had happily encountered on the road. Corolan was much bruised and stunned by the fall, but it was uncertain as to the extent of the injury. It was certain that he was seriously, if not fatally injured. He was speedily conveyed home and placed in his bed. Falkner could not be prevailed upon to leave the bed-side of his brother; and the mother—after the first shock had passed—remained by the unconscious Corolan as a ministering angel.

For several days and nights Corie suffered immensely, yet he seemed perfectly unconscious of what was passing around him. If he spoke, it was to warn his schoolmates from trespassing upon his rights. It was evident that, from a severe shock which the brain had received, that sensitive organ had suffered seriously. The physician informed the parents that, with proper treatment, their son might recover in the course of a few weeks. Falkner endeared himself still more to the parents by his unremitting attentions to Corie. If cold cloths were to be applied to the head of his brother, his willing hands performed the task. He would sit for hours and fan the fevered brow of his brother, and shed tears of sorrow at poor Corie's misfortune.

If he was overcome with fatigue and constant vigils, he could not be prevailed upon to leave the room, but would seek repose upon a couch by Corie's bed-side.— Blessed Falkner ! why should the dreams or the realities of life ever disturb the repose of one so pure as thou wert ?

One night, when Corie had revived, and there was a change in his condition for the better, Falkner—who had not left the room during the entire day—extended himself upon the couch and slept. At first he scarcely moved; but soon he became troubled as one in a frightful dream. Let us relate his dream, as told to his father the next day :

He dreamed that he was a child, quite young. He dwelt in a far-off clime. His father and mother were so fond of him, that they would scarcely permit him to leave their presence. He dwelt with them in a large, fine house—so unlike the one he had lived in so long. All the furniture was of the most costly kind. He was reminded of some scenes in the "Arabian Nights"—

yet, all the appearance of his dream had a semblance of reality. He dreamed that he was the owner of a large dog and a small canine pet, with which his hours were spent in much glee. The scene changed. He was sailing upon what appeared to him a broad river, with his father and mother. As the boat cut the rolling waves and the breeze fanned his infantile cheeks, he experienced sensations of pleasure. The scene changed again. He was playing beside the shore of that broad river with his nurse. Some fierce looking men landed close beside him. They seized him, struggling in the embraces of the nurse, and bore him off. So great was the struggle in his bosom, that he awoke, exclaiming, "Save me, father! oh! where is my mother?"

Mr. Manning rushed to the couch, and raised the boy up and observed that he was as pale as marble.

"Oh! father, where am I?" exclaimed Falkner, "I have had such a horrid dream."

"Pray relate it, son," said the father, "I am troubled to see you in such agony."

"Oh! I shudder to think of it. I cannot tell you now. Oh! father, tell me, am I not your son? At times, of late, I have heard you speak words whose meaning I have been at a loss to divine."

"Falkner, I should be a miserable man indeed, did I not esteem you more than a son. Come to this bosom, darling of my soul! Sleep, Falkner, go to your bed; mother and I will watch by the couch of Corie. You have much need of rest."

In a few days Corie was so much better that he was enabled to walk out upon the lawn, supported by the strong arm of his brother. Falkner was perfectly delighted to see the great improvement in the condition of his brother.

Day by day health and strength returned to Corie, and by the time vacation was at an end, the brothers were tired of sport, and joyfully resumed their studies under the astute supervision of the wise dominie Heflin.

Two years passed away, and still the brothers were at school. Falkner was now prepared for college. He was tall, muscular and active. His face was almost effeminately beautiful, while his dark, auburn hair rested in many a curl upon his shoulders. His soft, blue eye gave tokens of a greater degree of intelligence than is usually possessed by boys of his age.

Corie had not improved much in books, but he had grown rapidly. His disposition had slightly changed for the better. He had ceased to hate the dominie, and had learned to love Falkner. Within a few weeks it was decided that Falkner should be sent to the University of M——, only a few days' travel from home. As there was a preparatory school attached to the University, Corie, who had expressed a willingness to attend his brother, was to be Falkner's companion.

While Mrs. Manning is preparing for the departure of the sons, we will relate a few events which may not be uninteresting to the reader.

CHAPTER XVII.

IF we are particular at all times to respect the opinions of our friends, we will not be obliged to make useless apologies. The ancient philosophers supposed that next to wisdom, silence was the most commendable of virtues. If it were possible for our friends to remain silent and let our own actions speak for us, we might often be relieved of a world of trouble. Those who seek after popular favor are too often extolled to the skies by senseless wights whose opinions are worth not a *sous*, while the meritorious remain in comparative obscurity. It was thus the case with poor dominie Heflin, who had more talent than one in a thousand of those good men who are devoting their time and talents to the education of youth. He had remained in the background so long that it seemed as second nature to him to court obscurity. If he had been puffed by the press, as some are now-a-days who have not the scintilla of merit, it might have destroyed his usefulness. Besides being a very fine scholar, and a teacher whose merit was at least appreciated by those who were directly interested, he could survey land, draw up deeds, transcribe accounts, and, upon a pinch, write wills.

If the good dominie was not reaping the rich reward of his merits in this world, he was laying up his treasure

in Heaven—where neither moth nor rust can corrupt—
where thieves do not break through and steal. He
had surely performed his duty in teaching Falkner and
Corie. If the first-named had gained much by his wise
instructions, the second at least remembered some of
the wise tenets.

We said that the boys were nearly upon the point of
leaving for the University. Several days were wanting
to fill up the space ere the day appointed for their departure would arrive. The events of an hour or of a
day may decide the fate of an empire, or may raise or
lower a man who is struggling for supremacy.

One evening while the family were seated at the supper-table, one of the servants came hastily into the
house and stated that a man had been found in a fainting condition not far from the front gate. It was supposed by the servants that he had been thrown from his
horse, as his traveling sack had been found not far
from where he lay; and it was not at all probable that
a man so well clad as the unfortunate, would be found
performing his journeys on foot.

Mr. Manning and his sons left the table in haste, to
go to the relief of the man. They were followed by
the good domine, who happened to be spending the evening with the boys, just upon the eve of their departure.

Falkner being the swiftest of the party, arrived first
at the place where the wounded man lay. He raised
his head from the ground and discovered that the blood
was issuing from a wound which had doubtless been
caused by his head coming in contact with a hard sub-

stance upon the road-side. The man was evidently too
weak to hold conversation with the party, and was immediately taken to the house.

Falkner was forthwith dispatched for the family physician, who resided but a short distance from the homestead. While he was absent, the stranger was divested
of his apparel, and placed in a comfortable bed. Mr.
Manning had some experience in the treatment of
wounds and the management of invalids. The expert-
ness of the good dominic in staunching the blood and
applying bandages to the head of the unconscious man,
proved that he was equal to any emergency.

"What a finely formed man this is, friend Manning,"
said the classical dominic. "His hair, though partial-
ly gray, has the appearance of having been of a beautiful black color. Look at his handsome features. Old
age has not made this havoc; grief or dissipation has
taken time by the forelock."

"True, dominic," said the good man," circumstances,
at times, hasten the flight of old age. Have you not
read of men who have grown gray in one night?"

"I have, but those instances are rare. I read of a
man whose occupation was that of gathering the eggs
of birds which build their nests in the clefts of rocks
upon the sides of mountains and yawning precipices.
They were compelled at times to obtain the object of
their pursuit by perilous adventures. The father of the
boys, upon one occasion, was lowered several hundred
feet by a rope, in order that he might obtain the eggs
of numerous birds. He had despoiled the nests of many

of their treasures, not neglecting to break in upon the sanctity of the retreat of an eagle. The signal had been given for his sons to draw him up. He was gradually rising to the top of the steep precipice, when the mother eagle attacked him with all the fury of her bellicose nature. Drawing a hunting knife which he wore, concealed in a sheath, he dispatched the bird, but in so doing, he almost severed the cord by which he swung. It is said that he was perfectly gray when he was taken, fainting, from the noose in the rope, by his sons."

Just at this moment Falkner entered the room, followed by Doctor Gillis. A description of this singular individual may not be out of place. He was a man just above the medium height, rather thickly set. Judging from the wrinkles that illustrated his swarthy face, he might have been on the shady side of forty. His eyes were of a yellowish gray, and his head was nearly bald. His sandy whiskers were sprinkled with many gray ones. His clothes were cut after the most approved style, but his awkward gait and rustic air plainly indicated that he had not been used to fine apparel. He had evidently learned all his manners from observation.

"Good evening, Col. Manning," said the doctor. "Your obedient servant, professor Heflin." Here the doctor raised his gold-headed cane full in view of the company, and handing it and his hat to Corie, desired him to place them in one of the outer rooms. Pulling off his kid gloves, and taking a pinch of snuff from his silver snuff-box, this disciple of Æsculapius was prevailed upon to take a seat.

"Whom have we here, Col. Manning, that needs medical aid? Have you learned the circumstances by which he came to this accident? Have his wounds bled profusely? Do his pains seem to be acute?"

"It is difficult to answer all your queries at once, doctor; please examine him, and apply what remedies you can."

"But, Col. Manning," said the doctor, "it is entirely necessary to ask all these questions before we can diagnose a case. If Æsculapius himself were present— with all the remedies known to the healing art, or if I possessed all the healing herbs known to the wise ancients—nothing could be done for a patient without a proper knowledge of his disease. You are aware, also, Colonel, that the ancients were ignorant as to the use of the lancet. It was never thought the blood circulated, until Harvey demonstrated it conclusively to King Charles the First. When our class graduated, Colonel, in the city of Philadelphia, just twenty years ago, last June——"

"Do, if you please," interposed the Colonel, "go to the bed-side of the stranger and see what he needs. I do not desire to have a lecture upon Anatomy, Pathology or Surgery. You have told me all of those things more than one hundred times."

"Sir," said the doctor, much offended, "the fraternity of which I am a member should have some deference shown them. Do you suppose we burn the midnight lamp in vain? Do you consider the researches we make in science. nothing? Questions, sir, questions should be answered when put upon abstruse subjects."

"I beg pardon, doctor," said Mr. Manning, "but I do not see why you should make so much delay. Be kind enough to step to the bed-side and examine the patient."

The doctor being thus importuned, and having carried his point—which was to make a display of his learning before the dominie—went to the bed-side of the wounded man and felt of his pulse, which he reported as indicating much fever.

"Please request Mrs. Manning to send me some domestic goods for bandages, a plate, knife and spoon. and some warm water."

When those things were brought, the invincible knight of the pill-box divested himself of his coat, rolled up his sleeves, and made awful preparations for a display of medical skill. A small side-table was placed before him, and his saddle-bags were brought in by the ever-attentive Falkner.

"Now, Corie," said the doctor, "bring me a small quantity of treacle."

"A small quantity of what?" said the boy.

"Treacle, my lad; do you not know what treacle is?"

"I do not, sir," said the boy, "perhaps brother Falkner knows, he is about to leave for College."

"It is molasses, brother," said Falkner, "you are so fond of it and do not know the several names under which it is known!"

"If folks would use fewer big words and more plain English," said the boy, "we would have less use for wise doctors and learned teachers."

The doctor called for twenty things in a few minutes. Falkner and Corie were heartily tired of running to their mother for lint, pins, salve, thread, flannel, sugar and milk.

Mr. Manning and the dominie were afraid to open their mouths, dreading that the descendant of the god of the healing art would launch off into learned disquisitions upon Epilepsy, Catalepsy, or Hydrophobia.— Dr. Gillis thrust his pen-knife into a dozen vials, and extracted from each a small quantity of powder. In a very mysterious manner—known only to medical men—he mixed up a small compound, (thanks to the all-absorbing treacle;) having rolled it out to the proper length, he cut the compound into a dozen *fearfully looking slugs*, which were hastily formed into globules. An eye-witness would have pronounced them PILLS.

Oh! gentle reader, if you have the same horror of PILLS that we have, the very sight of a little round box with red sides, blue top and white bottom, will disturb your nerves.

The doctor looked up with a self-satisfied air, as much as to say, what a wonderful thing is the science of Pharmacy. He next mixed up several vial-fulls of mysterious liquids.

"Now, friend Manning," said the man of science. "let us examine the wounds of the stranger."

"With pleasure," said the host, whose patience had long since grown threadbare. "We should have done that at first, but doctors must have their way."

The doctor, when he had exploded all his gas, was

11

expert enough.   The bandages which the good dominie
had applied were removed, and the wound was washed
and properly dressed.   When the doctor left, the patient
was in a calm sleep.   The dominie and Falkner consented to watch by his bed-side, and administer the med-
icines at the proper time.

CHAPTER XVIII.

BLESSED is he that invented sleep—says some author
—it wrappeth one up as with a blanket. We can truly
say that doubly blessed is he who hath an opportunity
to sleep, and a good bed to lie upon. It is certain that
all of God's creatures do not enjoy healthy sleep; nor
is it within the power of every one to recline upon a
downy bed. Two of the sweetest bards that England
has ever produced, were so indigent that they could not
afford to rent rooms for lodgings. When the *cafes* were
closed at night, those authors with seedy garments,
were compelled to walk the streets of London until
dawn, unless generous friends invited them to their
houses. The great Fielding, whose quaint, classic style
of composition has rarely if ever been excelled, was so
beset with bailiffs and other pliant officers of the law,
that he could find but little rest either by night or day
Doctor Samuel Johnson, the wonder of his age, whose
articles in the Rambler set London in a blaze, was so
improvident of what money his great genius earned for
him, that he was frequently without the common necessaries of life.

Some authors suppose that an evil conscience has
many barriers to the incursions of Morpheus; but such
is not the case in every instance. Many a malefactor,

whose cruel hands have been imbrued in the blood of innocent victims, has slept soundly on the night previous to his execution.

Ill health, a hearty supper, the want of exercise, and irregular habits, will banish sleep from the eyelids of us all, whether we have good or evil consciences.

The stranger, whom chance had cast as an inmate in the house of Mr. Manning so unexpectedly to the members of the household, slept soundly and sweetly— (thanks to the good quality of the medicinal potations left in charge of the dominie and the tender-hearted Falkner.) The dominie, whose thirty years' occupation as teacher had taught him to sleep in his chair in an upright position, when the hour at which he usually retired arrived, could not keep himself awake. He placed his hands over his eyes as if endeavoring to induce the belief that he was in a state of meditation. Falkner was too well acquainted with his habits to believe that the good dominie was awake, when every signal he made was an indication that he was in the quiet retreat of Morpheus.

When the boy was warned by the significant strokes of the clock, that the hour had approached for the stranger to take his medicine, the good dominie was easily aroused from his meditative slumbers by a gentle touch.

"*Carissime puer, dormiebam,*" would be the only exclamation the sage would be heard to utter. He would rouse himself from his slumbers and exert all his efforts to assist the boy in performing the goodly task of administering the medicine of the renowned Gillis.

What a strange picture was there presented to an observer! Old age, with all the respect that is due it, was represented in the person of dominic Heflin. Middle age, or the prime of life, was truly impersonated in the character of the unknown, who lay stretched upon the bed of affliction. Everything that is concentrated in youth, hope and happiness, was impersonified in the person of the gifted youth, who sat by the bed-side of the sick man.

Falkner had arrived at the period of life when his mind had commenced expanding. He had read most of the works of the authors whose instructions are sought after. He longed to mingle with those whose path led to the temple of Fame. The instructions he had recieved from his teacher and from his dear father, were of such a character that he was not enabled to pause or linger by the wayside.

The good dominie slept, because it was his nature to do so. He could not have maintained the wakefulness of the watchful Falkner, because he had arrived at the period of life when age must succumb to the force of circumstances.

The map of life was spread out before our hero, with all its phases of good and evil. He thought it within his power to choose between the two extremes. Still there was an incubus which weighed upon his mind.— He had been early taught to consider that every man held his happiness in his own hands. If chance should cast the weight of the balances in his favor, it seemed as if Fate were upon his side : but might it not be mor-

ally true that the affairs of men are not entirely di
rected by chance ?

The dominic slept as sweetly as ever he did in the
halls of academus, Falkner smiled to see how the
good man endeavored to make it appear that he was only
in a meditative mood.

Falkner had arrived at that interesting period of life
when the mind is most active and the intellect is not
allowed to slumber. It was not his intention to remain
idle while there remained a chance for him to improve
his mind or to render himself useful to his fellow man.
Even whilst he watched by the bed of the unfortunate
man, he held a useful volume in his hands.

When the sick man was restless, the good boy was by
his side in an instant to attend to his wants. The
cooling drink was handed him by the attentive boy,
while the aged dominie slumbered in his easy chair.
The cold cloths were applied to the brow of the sick
man by the same tender hands ; and when day dawned
the vigilant boy was relieved from his watchful post by
Mr. Manning.

It is not exactly certain how long the good teacher
would have slumbered, had not the golden rays of the
morning sun aroused the erudite sage from his dreams.
When he rubbed his eyes, and observed that Falkner
was not present, he expressed some surprise ; but the
good dominie soon reflected that if there was any virtue attendant upon the vigils of the past night, himself
would share but little of it.

Mr. Manning had learned from his beloved boy that

the medicine had been regularly administered to the patient, (thanks to the watchfulness of Falkner.) But in order to cater to the vanity of the old teacher, Mr. Manning could not refrain from passing some compliments upon his good offices to the invalid.

When the dominie sought his home on that morning after breakfast, the astute Corolan ventured the remark that the teacher had imposed upon the goodness of his brother Falkner. He knew that it was a matter of impossibility for the teacher to maintain his watchfulness even by day. If the sick man had received any attentions at all, it was certain that dominie Heflin had not been a voluntary agent in rendering them.

The horse of the invalid had been arrested not far from the house by one of the servants. It was a matter of conjecture as to the social standing of the unknown ; yet, there would be time enough for the host to make all necessary enquiries when the convalescence of the guest would render it expedient.

In a very few days the stanger had improved so rapidly, that it was no longer necessary for him to remain in bed. He was a man of great intelligence, and was competent to interest his youthful acquaintances who sought his company. Corie was as much delighted at his anecdotes as Falkner was interested in his descriptions of his extensive travels.

Day by day the invalid's health improved ; still Falkner was his constant companion. One evening, when they were walking in the grove in front of the house, the following conversation passed between them :

"You say that you are about fifteen years of age.
Falkner, and have resided at this place from your infancy. Have you no recollections of having dwelt at
another home?"

"I am at a loss to comprehend the nature of your
enquiry," said the boy, "my father has been one of the
most indulgent of parents, whose love to me has been
unbounded. Pray tell me why you have propounded
the question?"

"I cannot tell you now, Falkner," said the stranger.
"we often propound questions which have but little or
no relevancy to the subject of conversation, yet subsequent events may bring obscure points to light."

"You distress me, sir," said the boy, grasping his
companion by the arm, "pray do not tantalize me with
wanton insinuations. If you know anything of my
early history, of which I am totally ignorant, in the
name of God, relieve my anxiety. I am prepared to
listen to any revelation, however disagreable it may be."

"Falkner," said the stranger, whose dark eyes beamed with a melancholy pleasure, as they rested upon the
boy, "there are some revelations we cannot make except
at the proper time. Do not allow what I have said to
distress you. It is true, you may think it unkind in me
to withhold from you that which it might be imprudent
in me to reveal. You see before you a stranger whom
your unremitting attentions during his illness, have
greatly endeared to you. Promise me faithfully that
you will reveal no part of this conversation to your father, or to any other person."

"If there is any truth in your insinuations, I can see no impropriety in asking my father for a full explanation upon every point relative to myself."

"Believe me, my young friend," resumed the stranger, "it is better for you to make me the promise I request. You are young yet, and do not know the ways of the world. I would not fill thy young mind with sorrow for the wealth of Crœsus. Do you see that star which the paling rays of the setting sun have given to our sight? Whilst the great lamp of day illumined the world, the inferior planets held no sway, yet the rays of that star have not been less brilliant. But see, as the sun hides his head behind the horizon, and the soft, mellow tints of the twilight are shed around us, each one of the small planets come out and sparkle with crystaline delight. Everything has been made by God for some wise purpose. We cannot foresee our own destinies; yet it is better for us to bide our time. Will you promise me not to relate what has occurred between us this evening?"

"It is strange that you should make such a request, my dear friend," said Falkner, "and I am at a great loss to comprehend you; still, if it is your desire—and doubtless you have your reasons—I will conceal my suspicions in my bosom."

"Noble boy," said the stranger, "take this, and wear it for my sake; it may, at some time act as an amulet to you."

Falkner received a beautiful gold chain, to which was attached a medal. The letters "C. R." were engraved upon it.

"Tell me your name," said Falkner, "I have never before asked it."

"Conrad Rodman—and if you should ever be reduced to the necessity of calling upon a friend for assistance, address me at H——."

CHAPTER XIX.

A few days subsequent to the one on which the conversation occurred between Falkner and Rodman, the latter departed from the hospitable mansion of Mr. Manning. He placed a letter in the hands of Mr. Manning, having exacted a promise from him that the seal should remain unbroken for the space of five years.— This, thought Mr. Manning, was a strange request; yet, he yielded to the urgent solicitations of Rodman, and the packet was carefully placed in a private drawer of his writing desk.

Mr. Manning was troubled in his mind. He suspected that the letter had especial reference to Falkner, who was as dear to him as his own son Corolan. Was Rodman the father of Falkner? and had chance thus thrown the father and son together? He formed a resolution to conceal from Falkner the fact that he was a foundling. He would make no revelations to the dear boy until he had taken his degree at the University. He fondly trusted that he would be enabled to explore the mystery before Falkner attained his majority.

The trunks of the boys were carefully packed by the good mother, whose tears of affection had bedewed the nice garments as she folded them and laid them in their proper places.

"I wonder why that black imp does not bring out the carriage," said Corolan, "here we have been waiting more than an hour. Master Falkner will cry his eyes out at parting with papa, if we do not hasten away from this place. Falkner, stay here with papa, and learn to be a farmer. You are already farther advanced in book learning than I ever expect to be, yet I am anxious to travel some."

"You must try and exercise more patience, my dear boy," said his father. "I have ordered the driver to wash the carriage and grease the wheels carefully. If you had as much love for your father as your brother exhibits upon all occasions, my cup of bliss would be full."

"Ah! father, you think I do not love you because I am too shame-faced to hug and kiss you and follow you up, as brother Falkner does. It is as much as I can do to let mother devour me with a thousand kisses each day."

"Promise me, Corie," said his mother, "that you will be a good boy, and listen to the advice of your brother. He loves you more tenderly than you do him. Oh! Corie, learn to imitate his good example and studious habits, and you will gladden the heart of your mother."

"I see the driver is coming with the carriage," said the father. "Here is your purse, Falkner; you will find in it enough money to pay your college bills for one year. You must give Corie some pocket-change as he requires it; but I need not advise you to be economical.

Good-bye, my sons ; write to me as soon as you get to the University."

The mother kissed the boys and shed many tears at their departure. Corie would have given birth to a few tears himself, but he had none to shed. As the carriage moved off, he thrust his head from the window and requested his father not to let black Dick ride his pony too hard. He wanted his fishing-poles kept in their proper place in the carriage house. Falkner was too sad to enjoy the rattling conversation of Corie. He was leaving his father, whom he almost worshipped.

" Come, brother, dry up those tears ; you cannot expect to be with papa always. He has placed me in your charge, but if you are to cry after this style, I shall think that you are not a safe guardian."

" Oh ! Corie, you are so unkind. Have you no tenderness in your nature ? You parted with father and mother as carelessly as if you expected to be gone but a few days."

"Master Falkner, you may yet learn some valuable lessons from me. I do not care much for books, and I thank my stars that I have but little of the girl's nature. You will pore upon the pages of a dry book as if your life depended upon your learning its musty contents. You have spent enough time in drawing and painting to have made you an adept in each branch of the art. Do you suppose that papa is a-going to let you set up as a painter or drawing master ?"

" You wrong painters and drawing masters, brother Corie, if you intend to cast a slur upon their professions.

If I thought I could arrive at distinction as an artist,
and father should happen to lose his fortune, I do not
suppose there would be any impropriety in my 'setting
up' as a painter."

"You misapprehend me, master Falkner; it is not
my intention to wrong any man wilfully. I should feel
very sorry indeed to see you laboring in a close room
with the brush and pencil- As for me, I love the sunshine and the cold, piercing winds. I am not disposed
to addle my brains by hard study. I care more for my
dogs, and gun, and fishing tackle, than for the knowledge that is contained in all the books in the world."

"It seems, Corie, that you are perfectly regardless
of the wishes of father and mother. They desire to
see you a studious boy. Why do you act so? You can
learn anything if you will only apply your mind to the
task. I shall be very much displeased with your conduct if you prove as inattentive to the instructions of
the teachers of the preparatory school as you have been
heretofore."

"Why do you wish to force me to study hard books
against my will? Do you ever expect to derive much
benefit from your incessant labor in translating Latin
and Greek? I can read and write tolerably well, and
with a few extra accomplishments, which I hope to gather by way of observation, I shall not despair of making
the most of life."

When the boys arrived at the town where they proposed to take passage in the stage, the carriage was
sent back home. The stage was not expected to leave

until towards night, and the lads had ample time to take
a stroll through the town. Falkner endeavored to point
out the objects of interest to his brother, who was perfectly delighted with everything he saw. How happy,
thought Corie, must they be who dwell in this beautiful
place!

"Look, brother Falkner, at that church yonder!
what is the use of that small house upon the top of it,
which runs up to so sharp a point? We have no such
churches in our old dull neighborhood. We are only
twenty miles from home, yet father has never thought
proper to let us come here before. If I do not improve
my time and see some strange sights before I return
home, then you may call me a dull boy."

"Look out, Corie," said Falkner, "those horses will
tramp you under their feet. You must not stand gazing idly at one object so long, or folks will think that
you have never seen a town before."

"People will think entirely right, brother, for we
have been kept at home like close prisoners. Look at
those beautiful chains in the window of that watch-
maker's shop. I see one almost exactly like the one
Mr. Rodman gave you."

"They are pretty indeed, Corie; if you will be economical, and not spend the money mother gave you, too
lavishly, I will put by some of mine and we will purchase one for you."

Every one that saw those interesting boys, was struck
with the beauty and manly bearing of the one, and the
independent, but easy manners of the other. When they

informed those who interrogated them that they were on their way to college, they were kindly assisted in purchasing their tickets. Corie was as much delighted at the idea of riding in the stage as Falkner was of knowing that he would soon be at the University, where he could apply all his energies to the acquisition of knowledge. The stage was crowded, but the boys obtained as good seats as any of the passengers. Corie was very talkative; but when the night was far advanced, he stretched himself upon the breast of his brother and slept as sweetly as if he had been in his own bed.

The good boy extended a parental care over his brother. He held him fast in his arms to protect him from harm.

"Bless your soul!" murmured Falkner, "you have but little love for any person, but for mother's sake I will protect you with my life. You shall want for nothing if it is in my power to assist you."

The attentions of the good boy did not escape the observation of the passengers. One of them said to Falkner:

"You take great care of your brother, I see."

"It is my duty," said the boy, "we are going to college, and mother has entrusted him to my care. If any harm should befall him, I would be loth to see the face of mother again. He desired so much to come with me that I consented to become his protector."

"You are a noble youth," said the elderly man, who had taken quite a fancy to Falkner. "I would give all the wealth I possess if I had a son like you. A long time ago I had a fair-haired boy stolen from me. I loved him so tenderly that I could scarcely trust him out of my sight. I have searched for him diligently over the United States—still my eyes have not yet rested upon him. I have received anonymous letters stating that my son was living"—— Here the grief of the noble looking man—who was probably about fifty years of age—choked up his utterance.

"How unfortunate!" said Falkner. "I trust you may yet recover your son. Have you no other children?"

I have not, my lad, but we have adopted a daughter of one of our deceased friends. She is beautiful and charming, but can the place of my son be filled? What is your name?"

"Falkner Manning," said the boy. "My father dwells at Oak-Lawn, in the county of S——."

The conversation between Falkner and the stranger was very interesting and entertaining, especially to the latter, who, on parting with the boy, declared to a friend that he was the most interesting youth he had ever seen.

Falkner and Corolan arrived at their destination in two days from the time they started from home. The good youth had been so well prepared, (thanks to the kindness of dominie Heflin,) that he entered the Freshman class very easily. Corie was entered as an academician. He was permitted to share the room of his brother. If Corie had been delighted with the large towns and small villages he had passed through, he was completely charmed at the appearance of the magnifi-

12

cent edifices on the Campus.   Falkner had much difficulty in directing the attention of his brother to his
books.   When he had arranged his room and been received as a regular student of the University, he wrote
the following letter to his father :

CHAPTER XX.

"University of M——, August 1st, 18—.

"*My dear and much beloved father:* Brother Coric has just ceased his noise in the room, and is making preparations for retiring. It is with unfeigned pleasure that I attempt to write an epistle to you. Be so kind, dear father, as to excuse any imperfections that you may find in this letter, as it is the first I have ever attempted to write to you. I can now appreciate some of the lectures the good dominie used to deliver to our class upon the subject of composition. I was too young to comprehend the meaning of the technical terms the good man made use of, but his tuition, even upon those abstruse subjects, may yet benefit me.

"It has been scarcely ten days since I parted with you, yet it seems as if an age had passed since that time. I thought I loved you dearly while at home, but my affection has increased doubly of late. Coric has been advising me by all means to abandon the idea of remaining here and return immediately to your embraces. It is childish in me to be writing to you in any such style but I can not help it.

"To say that I am pleased with the University and everything appertaining to it, is but to confess the truth. I have a finely furnished room, with as many useless

luxuries as your fatherly care allows me at home.—
Corie sometimes desires extra attention, but I have
assured him that I would not consent to spend more
money than is absolutely necessary; therefore I have
only engaged the services, together with the aid of several of the students, of one negro, whom the Faculty
permit to wait upon the students.

"I must give you a short description of my examination. When I had presented myself for admission, the
old professors, (bless their wise pates!) ogled me through
spectacles which seemed to possess the sense of seeing.
I could scarcely withstand the gaze of the wise men;
but I tried with my utmost powers to preserve my equa-
nimity. How my timid heart throbbed when, in company with forty boys, I was called upon to recite. My
tongue became dry and silent. I could scarcely articu-
late one word; but, remembering your advice, I composed myself, and commenced reading one of the
Eclogues of Virgil. I was even surprised at my own
success, and when I sat down I perceived that the professor who was conducting the examination was pleased
with my effort. I had but little difficulty in convincing
each one of the Faculty that I was prepared for entry
into the Freshman class.

"I have some difficulty in keeping brother in our room
at night; yet I trust by entreaties and promises he may
disappoint our expectations. Corie has some pride, and
if I can operate upon that, I shall not despair of suc-
ceeding in arresting his attention and directing it to his
books.

"I have engaged a gentleman who gives lessons in painting, to instruct me. I am heartily delighted with his tuition, and trust that I may be enabled to paint your and mother's portraits when I come home in vacation. If you think the expense is unnecessary, the painter's instructions shall be instantly dispensed with.

"Kiss mother a thousand times for me, and let her return each salutation. Tell her that the beautiful ruffled shirts she made me are admired by all the students.— Corie has torn his new coat and almost spoiled his vest, yet I have hopes that he will quit his sportive tricks.

"Good night, dear father; may angels guard you by day and night; remember your Falkner always in your prayers. Remember that you have ever a dutiful son in your FALKNER."

When Mr. Manning received the above letter from Falkner his eyes were filled with the tears of affection. How could he ever make the revelation to the boy that he knew must be made sooner or later! If Corolan possessed one-half the talent that Falkner did, or if he was endowed with the same good disposition which rendered Falkner so amiable, then he might consent to tell Falkner that he was not the brother of Corolan. He believed that Falkner suspected that there was some obscurity about his birth, but he hoped that the boy would ever consider him as his own dear parent.

The letter which Rodman had left with such strict injunctions weighed heavily upon his mind. He desired to know the information those mystic pages might reveal to him; yet he remembered that he had given his pledge not to break the seal until the five years had expired.

Was he bound to keep his pledge with a man who was unknown to him—one who owed him the preservation of his life? Mr. Manning felt that it was wrong even to violate pledges given to an enemy, although the moral law would have borne him out in that. But he had pledged himself not to break the seal of the letter for a specified time, and, come weal or woe, his word should be kept. He knew Falkner's confiding, yet independent disposition, and almost shuddered at the consequences attendant upon the revelation. He was ignorant as to the parentage of the boy. He could never desert Falkner, but the half of his estate should be offered him! Would he accept it? That was the point that troubled Mr. Manning. Corolan was a gay boy, whose love or attachment for an individual was not worth a fig; yet, he was Mr. Manning's only child. He loved him because he was his son—he loved Falkner for himself alone.

———

"OAK-LAWN, August 15th, 18—.

Dear Son: Your kind letter reached me a few days since by due course of mail, and as you request it, I hasten to dispatch you an early answer. I rejoice exceedingly that you and Corie arrived safely at your place of destination. I am sorry you did not relate the particulars of your trip, which, I doubt not, were highly interesting to you and your brother.

You will discover, my dear son, that the world abroad is quite different from what it is at home. In your situation as student you will not be forced to contend with the world except in miniature. When you shall have grown older, and the leaden shadows of mature age have thickened around you, then you may realize the responsibilities of life. Beware of those who flatter you; they are often foes to you, rather than friends. They may seek to devour you with kind words and endearing phrases, yet their actions are like a sepulchre which, though white, smooth and beautiful without, is filled with dead men's bones. Above all things, shun the society of him who is devoid of integrity. The baneful influence of such a one is more to be dreaded than a contact with the Upas tree. Truth is a Heavenly virtue which shines resplendant under all circumstances; like pure gold, the more it is burnished the brighter it will glisten. Truth dwells at the bottom, because the purest foundations are deepest. Truth is located in the middle of every circle, for the reason that it is equally distant from every arc.

"Be plain and easy in your manners, so that every one may claim your frendship. Borrow not from your friends. but lend to those that are needy. Be neat in your dress. for the WORLD may judge you by your apparel. Learn while you are yet a youth to value the precepts of the Bible—that great Book of Life. Let it be as dear to you as the apple of your eye, though all inferior books be neglected.

"Be kind to your brother and keep him within the paths of rectitude.

"God bless you, is the prayer of your father

THEODORE MANNING."

CHAPTER XXI.

We shall not attempt to relate the particulars of a boy's actions at college, as a narrative of that kind is not interesting to the general reader. A few words upon college government may not be inappropriate.— One of the objections to sending boys to college, is that they learn bad habits. If no restraint is thrown around them by strict discipline, it is not to be supposed that a large number of boys and young men will remain long in any Institution without diverging from the path of rectitude. Those that are studious, modest and reserved, may withstand the thousand and one temptations which allure so many good youths from the paths of virtue, and plunge them into the depths of misery. What are familiarly known as college scrapes generally originate from a desire on the part of a few headstrong boys to have what they term "a little fun." Sport, like dissipation, when too freely indulged in, is a dangerous thing. The passions of boys, when once aroused, are more violent than those of men, and more difficult to allay. It is generally the fault of discipline that renders disagreeable occurrences among students frequent. Moral suasion may do much in effecting a change towards amelioration, yet there are some boys whom the most stringently enforced rules often fail of bringing into subjection. It is a fact, that outrages upon buildings and the furniture are often perpetrated by students who are desirous of attesting their aversion to certain members of the Faculty, thus casting odium upon every member of the college. Numbers of boys have been victimized by designing ring-leaders who had objects of their own to accomplish. When once the disturbance ceases, the participants are generally penitent; yet, if harsh measures are used in enforcing the penalties of the violated law, the pride of the students, in many instances, when arraigned before the Faculty for misdemeanors, will prevent them from making confessions or of pledging themselves to offend no more.— Would it not be better for the Faculty to use mild measures in enforcing the laws, by appealing to the honor of the student? Let the laws be executed with firmness, impartiality and moderation, with an eye single to the welfare of the Institution, thus exhibiting a desire upon the part of the Faculty to act upon each case in the capacity of an unbiased tribunal, then there will be an alacrity upon the part of every student to respect the laws.

Frequent lectures by the President upon moral subjects, will tend, in an exceedingly great degree, to direct the mind of the student to that course of training which will prepare him for usefulness and induce him to eschew the evil counsels of the wicked.

It has been unwisely urged upon the Trustees of Universities to construct their laws requiring the students to obtain their board and lodging at the houses of those who reside near the campus—thus using the rooms of the University as recitation halls alone. Young men will not submit to being placed under the surveillance of a professor or tutor; neither will the latter consent to play the part of a pedagogue or usher. Young men will have occasional frolics, and it is better for them to confine their REVELRIES within the *sanctity* (?) of their own rooms than to invade the underground regions of a GIN COURT, imbibe the unhealthy potations of *suspicious* decanters, treat forty *sovereigns* in the persons of hangers-around, learn billingsgate phrases from idlers, get *gentlemanly drunk*, boisterous and warlike—and lastly, be conducted by the police to a "LOCK-UP." In a word, it is as easy a task to conduct the affairs of a State as to govern one hundred and fifty young men, with one hundred and fifty gold watches, one hundred and fifty Colt's Repeaters, one hundred and fifty bottles of choice "Old Otard," one hundred and fifty dulcineas, one hundred and fifty fine suits making at the tailors' shops, one hundred and fifty dollars a year of pocket-money, and one hundred and fifty miles from their one hundred and fifty fathers, who are satisfied to let their dear sons have their own way. If the dear boys bring home a "SHEEP SKIN" at the end of four years, (which they are unable to read) the delighted fathers feel as happy as so many presidents.

Dear reader, is it not one hundred and fifty wonders that the Faculty, students and sheep-skins all get along as harmoniously as they do? Bless all their dear souls, (not the sheep skins) let us pray for them and drop the

subject. Colleges are good places to sow *wild oats* in.
We are decidedly in favor of colleges with all their imperfections.

Falkner and Corolan were sitting in their room one
night soon after their advent to the University of M———.
The former was busily engaged in reading one of the
Odes of Horace, while the latter was looking at the
pictures in a book which one of the boys had lent him.

"Come, brother," said Falkner, "do lay aside that
ridiculous book and let me teach you your lesson.
Come, now, you remember what I promised you about
the chain, do you not?"

"Falkner," said the boy, "I do not think I shall ever
be able to learn Latin. I see but little sense in it;
can you not prevail upon the teacher to let me skip it?"

"You talk so strangely, Corie, that I am astonished
at you. It is impossible for you to enter College without a thorough knowledge of Latin and Greek."

The boys were cut short in their conversation by a
knock at the door. Corie opened it, and admitted about
a dozen boys, who had come to pay the new-comers a
visit. Falkner welcomed them to his room and desired
them to be seated.

"Falkner Manning," said one of the party, "we are
going to have a little 'burst up' to-night. You and
your brother must be of the party, since you are strangers; besides, we have not initiated you into the mysteries of college life yet."

"You must excuse me, my friends," said Falkner; "I
do not desire to go out to-night. I promised father that

I would be studious, and not engage in any sports forbidden by the laws of the University. I must prepare my lessons to-night, or my standing will not be high at recitations to-morrow."

"You talk as if you disdained our sport, Manning," said the spokesman of the party; "we are not used to having our mandates disobeyed. You will find it much to your advantage to come with us without compulsion."

"With all due deference to your sports—of which I know nothing—please allow me to remain in my room with my brother, unmolested."

"You both shall go with us," said several, who appeared to become excited all at once.

"You cannot and shall not force us," said the resolute boy.

One of the boys took hold of Corolan, who was in for the sport, while several of them advanced towards Falkner to coerce him into submission. The latter pushed them aside, and rushed to rescue Corolan from the strong youth who was marching off with him.

"Put down my brother, sir, or you shall feel my vengeance," said Falkner.

The command was not obeyed, and Falkner seized the boy, and before assistance could be offered by the astonished crowd, Corolan was rescued, and the boy whom Falkner had encountered, was hurled violently from the room into the street. The other boys were dreadfully enraged at the conduct of Falkner, and gathered around to conquer him. Falkner's blood was up, and he bade them stand off. One of the boldest approached to contend with him, but he was soon thrown from his footing. A second and third shared the same fate. Falkner would have been overpowered in a short time had not some of the professors come to his assistance. The baffled students fled in all directions—some with slight bruises upon their heads and faces.

When Falkner explained the cause of the disturbance to the professors, they were astonished at his prowess and determination to conform to the laws of the University.

The next day the "invaders" were arraigned before the Faculty for their misdemeanors and severely reprimanded. Some of them would have been expelled or suspended, had not the good Falkner pleaded for them.

The boys pronounced Falkner a noble fellow, and from that time he was regarded as a general favorite.

CHAPTER XXII.

WE love to see modesty in a boy. It is an ennobling virtue which should commend itself, at times, even to men. We are disposed to consider ourselves free from this fault, simply for the reason that charity sometimes begins at home. Parents owe it to society to educate their children properly *at home*. Then we should have fewer self-constituted critics upon manners and fashions; fewer masters of ceremonies at social parties, and fewer nonsensical debates in political meetings. Esquire Lighthead says to his son, "do not let any of them turn you down, my boy; hold up your head and be a man; tell folks that your father has fifty negroes—makes one hundred and fifty bales of cotton. Here is a dollar for you to buy whatever you please." That parent is inducing precocity in his son, which may prepare him for misery. Teach a boy that he is upon an equal footing with his fellows, and superior to none except for his moral worth—he is then prepared to commence the world aright. If a boy is not taught that it is wrong to speak improperly to men, especially to old ones, he will grow up a man who will be compelled to learn politeness in the costly school of experience.

Mr. Manning had endeavored to perform his duty in this respect; still he had failed to observe the good effects of his precepts as applied to Corolan; but Falkner readily conformed to every requirement. If his father had not neglected the sage counsels of Solomon, Corolan might have been a better scholar and more exemplary in his general deportment. If the froward boy had been moderately chastised with a slender branch of an umbrageous beach tree, when all persuasive arguments had been exhausted, it is doubtful whether Falkner would have excelled him. Boys may be punished moderately without resorting to cruel measures; yet, if they cannot be conquered without it, give them the rod freely.

"Corie, you have less modesty than any boy I have ever seen. Your teacher has already complained to me about your conduct. He says you are intolerably impertinent, and hard to control. If you do not change your course of conduct, I shall be reduced to the painful necessity of reporting you to father."

"Brother Falker, I shall become angry with you if I am to be thus lectured by you. I do not care what the teacher says. I intend to do just as I please, in spite of him and you."

"What I dislike mostly in your conduct is, that when any of the students call upon me, you speak to them so harshly that they are forced to withdraw—fearful of offending me by entering into a controversy with you. Do not brag upon father's wealth, and hold yourself up so stiffly; the wiser portion of the students will laugh at you. Suppose we are rich, is that any reason for you to boast of it? Now, brother, once for all, I shall

not allow you to spend so much money. You want me
to buy a fine suit of clothes for you, because one of the
boys has told you that you need them. Before I order
our Winter suits, I must write to father and get his advice. Only yesterday you spent one dollar for fruits,
which you distributed among those noisy boys whom
you bring in here to annoy me."

"Come, master monitor, if I may be allowed thus to
salute your reverence," said Corie, who had much wit;
"I am heartily tired of your sermons—or whatever you
call them. I must have another suit of clothes, as the
last suit old rustic Threadneedle made for me do not
fit; besides, they are not exactly in the latest style.—
I must let you into one of my secrets, brother, which
your sense of honor will enjoin upon you to keep. You
remember, last Sabbath, we went to Church, and do
you remember seeing a pretty girl, who sat in the pew
across the aisle from us? Well, she looked at me, and
I looked at her, and we both looked at each other. I
think she is smitten with me, Falkner, and if I can
make a conquest of her, your brother Corie may not
have come to College in vain. I learn she is quite
wealthy, and have been informed that she is anxious to
see me."

"Come, my youthful Adonis," said Falkner, "you
are thirteen years of age, and are making your arrangements to commence assuming the sphere of manhood.
Why bless my soul! I expect you will imitate the actions of King Richard the First and his brothers, who
rebelled against their father, and tried to wrest the

sceptre from his hands, ere they had arrived at the age of puberty. If you have any notions of marrying this young lady this Winter, I hope you will not sell out father's land and negroes without consulting him. You may have my share in advance, if you will only sell that and your portion."

"You are almost too pure for this earth, brother," said Corie; "I fear I may wake up some morning and find that you have been translated to a better world.— You must not take your flight until I have learned more wise words from your lips, for I can assure you that I shall never be able to learn anything from books. Besides, I shall need your assistance in supplying myself with a few phrases or set speeches to be used when I go out to see my dulcinea, as you and father would call her. Now, Falkner, if you will just consent to lend me your assistance, and write my love letters for me—be sure to put in some French words—I do not know but that I will give you the black pony and one of my choice fishing-poles."

"Now, Corie, I have heard enough of your nonsense for one night. Just close upon your love affairs, and apply yourself to your books. I never heard such non sense as sometimes falls from your lips."

"Very good, master Falkner, I will obey you this time; but I shall resume the discussion of the subject on to-morrow evening at early candle-light."

Falkner possessed more control over his brother than any other person, with the exception of his mother, and knew exactly how to appeal to his sense of pride He

13

was exceedingly kind to him, and had never been known to strike him. If he had anything in his possession which the boy wanted, he immediately resigned it to his hands. What a marked difference was there in the deportment of Falkner to Corolan, as compared with that of some older brothers. Love begets love, it is said, and there is nothing truer than that unkind intercourse between brothers engenders hatred which even the wisdom of age and the charity of reason can never dispel.

It seemed to be natural with Corolan to oppose every thing that pleased his brother, so different were their dispositions. Falkner knew the habits of Corie so well, that he rarely opposed him except in matters of great importance. He desired to continue the rules by which his parents had governed the refractory boy. He loved his brother, because it was evident that the disagreeable boy had but few friends, and it was entirely uncertain how long he would retain them.

The preparatory school was situated in a shady grove convenient to the Campus. Falkner made it an invariable rule to be near the Academy when the boys were dismissed for the day, in order that he might join his brother and induce him to take a walk. He thought by pursuing this course Corolan might be freed from many temptations, and finally reclaimed from the error of his ways. Falkner was almost a man in statue, though he was scarcely sixteen years of age; yet he was very juvenile, and almost effeminate in appearance, and it seemed perfectly consistent for him to be Corolan's pro-

tector. Corolan was small for one of his age, though
compactly built; he was hardy and perfectly prepared
to encounter hardships.

"Now, Falkner, if you desire to walk for a wager,
suppose you mark off a circuit and let me choose my lo-
cation and keep time—for it is evident to my mind that
I cannot keep pace with you, and I have just consulted
my legs upon the subject, and find them unwilling to
enlist in the contest."

"I beg pardon, brother; I have been so accustomed
to walking with father that I had forgotten that your
short legs were contending with mine."

"You are perfectly excusable, my young philosopher,
but you must not offend again after the same style.—
What did father say about the clothes we should buy
this Winter? I am getting extremely anxious to appear
before my dulcinea."

"Am I to be tortured thus every day about your dulcinea? Surely you must imagine yourself a youthful
Don Quixotte. If you had the black pony here, I
doubt not but that you would order a suit of mail and
go out upon an expedition. Father writes to me to
order a new suit of clothes for you and one for myself.
I will not purchase any for myself, but will order a supply of paints and drawing materials in lieu of the same.
We will go now to the store and make the purchases.
What color do you prefer for your suit, Corie?"

"If I am to choose for myself," said the delighted boy,
"I will select black cloth for the coat, blue casimere for
the pants, and buff cloth for the vest."

"Here is the place, now, Corie, for us to make our purchases. Here seems to be everything we need; so let us walk in and see what the merchant has."

"You must let me make my own selections, then, and allow me to do the principal part of the talking. At times I will ask your opinion, but you must coincide with me. I have not had a real good spell of talking in two weeks, and I wish to exercise my voice."

"Have your own way this time," said Falkner. "I hope you will not keep me witing until dark, nor should you worry the merchant."

"That is fair for once in your life, brother, just give me your paw upon that," said Corolan, as they entered the finely furnished store.

Corolan displayed his taste, exercised his lungs and the patience of his faithful brother, who paid the bill to the irated merchant, whom the young Adonis had offended more than once before the purchases were made. The goods were left at the tailor's with directions to have the suit made up after the most approved style.

CHAPTER XXIII.

WHEN Corolan received his new suit of clothes, he was so much delighted that the room could scarcely contain him. He stripped himself to the skin, washed with brown Windsor soap and arrayed himself with as much pride as an Eastern prince. Falkner did not appear to notice him at all, for fear the boy might become dissatisfied with the clothes and cast them aside. Coric was really a fine looking boy, with as much pride as ever falls to the lot of mortals. He was one of those strange beings who believe everything made especially for their use, and that they are formed to receive attentions without rendering services for the same. He walked up to the mirror, surveyed himself a few moments, cast a glance at his brother, who did not think it prudent to look in that direction, and making the discovery that Falkner was not watching him, the vain lark commenced the task of copying the mode of arranging his hair and cravat from the style of his brother. He tried to make his hair curl like Falkner's, but it seemed impossible for him to do so. After several ineffectual attempts at imitation, he adopted his own plan. He next endeavored to tie his cravat like Falkner usually did, but made an utter failure. "I know what I can do," murmured the boy: "I can brush off as much dust as Falkner can, wash my skin as clean, if not as white as his, and can use up as much cologne as he can, but to save my life I cannot look half as respectable as he does. Blame the fine looking fellow! everything comes perfectly natural to him, yet he is as indifferent to his charms as I am vain of my silly attempts at display."

"Brother Corolan," said Falkner, "you look very charming in your fine new dress; I suppose you are going out to see your dulcinea?"

"You are rather fast this evening, Falkner; I am only trying on the clothes to see whether they fit me or not. I am rather inclined to think they do not suit me, since you are so well pleased with them."

"Turn around Corie," said the boy; "I had *not* observed them very closely; I think now that the coat is rather loose in the back for you, and the sleeves are a trifle too tight just above the elbows. Your pants do not stand out as they ought to, and the vest is rather short for you."

"If that is your opinion, I am perfectly satisfied to wear them, as our ideas upon dress are as different as the poles. This coat sets as easily upon me as my skin, and it is the only one I ever had that suited me in the least. Look at the collar how smoothly it lies, and the waist fits snugly up. Nothing can be more charming than the pants, and as for the vest, it is a paragon of beauty. Oh! I shall surely make a conquest of my sweetheart now."

"I hope you are not going to visit her without ever

having formed her acquaintance, Corie; for if I am not egregiously mistaken, you have not yet seen her except at church. Do wait and exercise some patience, brother, or you will force your friends to laugh at you. The students are to give a party very soon; it may be possible that your intended will be present. For the balance of the evening please take up your books and endeavor to learn your Latin lesson."

"You are surely relating a fable to a deaf man now, Falkner, for I shall have no use for the dead languages, having but little desire to converse with ghosts. Do you suppose Cicero, if he should rise from the dead, could understand you and professor Graymont? I have never been so completely worried out in my life as I was one night last week. The antique professor and your ancient self clattered away at the verbs, adjectives and pronouns, until I almost wished that the spacious earth was one voluminous Latin Grammar and you and he were the only inhabitants upon it."

"That is very uncharitable in you, brother, since I have been so kind as to induce father to buy that suit of clothes for you. Do I not literally stuff your lessons down your throat? You do not try to receive them through the channels of reason. I see plainly that you must learn everything by imitation or frequent repetition."

"That is sufficient, brother; you are putting me fast to sleep; I feel the leaden god, as you and professor Graymont call him, drawing his sable curtains around me. *Vale*, Falkner, *somnus venit. et Corolan, tuus carissimus frater dormit.*"

The wild, but brilliant lad, tired himself completely out before he ceased talking, and having disrobed, went to bed to dream of his dulcinea, the black pony and the new watch his mother had promised to send him. Falkner was heartily glad to be rid of the noise, and commenced studying his lesson in good earnest. The clock struck one that night before the studious young man sought rest in sleep.

We have before remarked that Falkner was the favorite of the students. His room was the trysting place for those who were at all inclined to be studious. One boy frequently performs the task of translating the lessons for the entire class, and Falkner was chosen for that purpose. If he could not read an intricate sentence, solve a mathematical proposition or elucidate an abstruse question in rhetoric or logic, the professors were applied to. It was rarely that the learned boy failed to give entire satisfaction upon any point.

Time flew by rapidly and the end of the first year of Falkner's college life was approaching. He had easily maintained the first position in the class, though much of his time had been spent in amusing and instructing his brother. He had redeemed the promise he made to Corie relative to the chain. The virgin gold links supported the beautiful watch his mother had sent him, thanks to Falkner's liberality. His dulcinea had not been as easily victimized as he imagined, yet he had some hope of obtaining her love by another year. If she had bluffed him, the secret was carefully kept by the astute lad.

Falkner had learned to write verse, and had been complimented by the professors. He was pronounced to be the brightest student that had ever entered the University. The following letter to his father may be read with interest:

"UNIVERSITY OF M——, June 1st, 18—.

"*Dear Father :* I am rejoiced to inform you of the change in brother Corolan's habits. It is said that drops of water will eventually wear away the hardest stones, so will a dull mind receive instruction by frequent repetition. I had almost despaired of Corolan's ever being able to master the rudiments of the Latin language, but it is true he has made wonderful progress during the last few months.

"Do not blame me, dear father, if you discover that I have allowed him more money than you directed me to give him. I think he is entirely too fond of dress, yet without a stimulus of some kind he would not have been satisfied to remain as a student with boys who are so finely attired.

"I am truly beset with temptations, yet I strive to remember your counsels, trusting that I may do no wrong.

"If I win the esteem and praises of the virtuous and good, I shall be confident that I have done my duty. The older I become, the more I am impressed with the obligations I am under to respect the laws of the Supreme Being who upholds and sustains us by His superior goodness. Some of the students pretend to be atheists, but their very assertions are confuted by the arguments they use. I fear that brother's young mind may become imbued with their false philosophy, yet I shall battle against those influences with all my might.

"I am not a believer in dreams, but I do have some very strange scenes presented before me at times whilst I sleep. You remember the singular, yet painful, dream I had when brother was so dangerously ill? I have had a repetition of the same nocturnal visitation again of late. I shall not allow it to weigh upon my mind; but why should I conceal it from you? I do think I shall experience strange vicissitudes of fortune at some period of life.

"You have often warned me against the use of ardent spirits. A few days since, brother and I were invited to a party given at the house of one of the Faculty. Wine was plentiful at the table; still I drank only one glassfull; I am sorry to say that Corolan was not so abstemious. At the risk of revealing secrets, I must relate a funny little circumstance: I observed that Corolan was drinking as much as any of the students, and I went to him and remonstrated with him, but all to no effect. One of the members of my own class who has taken quite a fancy to brother, was acting as his chaperon on that occasion. He took a fresh bottle of champagne and opened it. He desired the boys to hold their glasses for another draught. Brother was so completely under the influence of what he had already drank, that he mistook the stopple of a decanter for a wine-glass, and held that to the boy to be filled with the intoxicating beverage! I managed to get him to our room before it was discovered that he had become too merry. He has promised me that he will not drink more than I do at any future party, and you know that Corie will keep a pledge sacred when it is once given.

"I will write to you again in a few days and enclose some verses which I am now composing.

"Yours in love,

Falkner."

CHAPTER XXIV.

"UNIVERSITY OF M——, June 5th.

"*My dear Father:* I promised, in my last letter, to send you some verses, which I now enclose. I trust that you may not criticise my first effort at a long poem too closely. I have not shown it to any person, though often tempted to ask the advice of one of the professors.

"Corie thinks that I will be a poor man some of these days, because I am learning to paint, and have a fancy for poetry. He says he has peeped into the pages of some moon-struck authors himself, when he thought no one was watching him, and he has learned that most of the bardlings died poor. He is a rare boy, whose like has never yet been seen by me.

"Request mother to make a beautiful ruffled shirt for me by the time I get home, and I will bring her something pretty. I will not worry you with a long letter, fearing that you may be tired out with the 'HERMIT'S TALE.'

"THE HERMIT'S TALE.

"Dark was the night; the wind blew shrill and loud;
The rain descended from the angry cloud;
The mountain trembled 'neath the thunder's sound,
And Nature's echoes filled the groves around.
The stately oaks, (the forest's giants old.

Beneath whose shades for countless years untold,
The hero, sage, or Indian warriors wild
Had planned their fights, or on their fair ones smiled,)
Dark, to the sky their stalwart branches bend,
While torrents through the leafy domes descend.
The wolf went howling to his rocky lair,
Led onward by the lightning's fiery glare;
Nor stopped he at the hermit's sainted cell—
That holy one whom all men loved so well.
Long years had passed since first the hermit came—
None knew from whence, nor had they learned his name.
But this they knew: by either night or day,
If luckless wight should on that mountain stray,
And wander to the hermit's sainted cell,
He lingered long, and every word that fell
From lips which only deigned to speak in prayer,
Was hoarded up as some prized relic rare.

" Fierce raged the storm; young Tibald's fiery steed,
Scared by the lightning, put forth all his speed;
And rushing from the road and through the dell,
Climbed the rough peak and reached the hermit's cell.
The holy father, on his knees in prayer,
Was asking aid from Heaven; his every care
Or ill of life was cast upon his beads;
Those numbered he in fervency. His deeds
Were known to Heaven; may his prayer be heard:
Who trusts in prayer believes God's holy word.

" Long gazed young Tibald, then, with wild delight;
Still knelt the hermit at his altar bright,
Nor ceased he from his fervent Vesper prayer
Till all his beads were told. His knees were bare
From oft reclining on the flag-stone cold;
Around his neck was hung a cross of gold.
A sable robe around his form was thrown,
And wooden sandals on his feet were worn.
Three waxen candles shed their mellow light
Within the cell upon that stormy night.
The hermit beckoned Tibald to a seat—

A rustic stool whereon his sacred feet
Had oft reclined when stretched upon his bed,
And leaden shadows 'round the cell were spread.

  "'Holy hermit! one night within thy cell
I pray thee let a wayworn traveler dwell;
My limbs are wet and chilled with drenching rain;
Dark is the night and trackless is the plain.
My charger, frightened at the thunder's sound,
Forsook the road and up the mountain wound.'
Then from a recess in the rocky wall
The hermit brought a chest compact and small;
A secret spring threw back the iron lid,
And garments fine within the chest lay hid.
'Long years have passed,' the holy father said,
'Since on these clothes mine aged eyes were laid;
I could a tale, young man, to you unfold—
But no; my secret to the silent grave
With me must go—ave Maria, save."
Then took he from the chest the garments rare
And robed his strange young guest with studied care.
Bright glowed the flames within the sacred cell;
The smoking meat sent forth a savory smell;
The red wine sparkled in the goblet bright,
And soon a festive board made glad the sight.
'The time has come when from this aching breast
My secret must come forth; my soul will rest
On earth no more until is brought to light
The hidden scenes of that eventful night.'
The hermit gazed upon his youthful guest,
Who, in the old, but princely, garments dressed,
Was seated at the well-filled, rustic board.
The rosy wine was in the goblets poured—
The rosy wine long in the larder stored.

  " The feast was o'er; the table moved from sight;
Still raged the storm, and doubly dark the night;
Then crossing thrice himself with pious care,
The holy hermit knelt again in prayer.
His prayer was ended; then he sought his guest.

And 'round his waist his stalwart arm was pressed.
'Oh! let me gaze upon thy youthful face,
My prince, my boy; methinks I now can trace
My own resemblance in thy features fair;
My long black curls were like thy raven hair
When first the regal crown with diamonds spread.
By pious hands was placed upon my head.
My royal spouse across the ocean came,
And lit the altar with love's holy flame;
When in my arms I pressed her form so fair—
Dark were her eyes and black her flowing hair—
My wide dominions dwindled into nought,
Compared to her. Could love like hers be bought?
Swift passed the days, and sweet the rosy hours
Unheeded, flew. One eve within the bowers
Whose leafy dome would scarce admit the light
Of that bright orb, the silvery lamp of night,
We sat and listened to the nightingale
Repeating to her mates her plaintive tale;
My soul was filled with love, and grief, and pride;
I knew not why, for in my royal bride
My soul was centered, yet my heart was sad;
Such fervent love had well nigh made me mad.
I could have dwelt with my sweet spouse forever.
(But cruel fate from her my love did sever;)
I could have dwelt beneath that bower so bright
And wished that day were one eternal night—
One night of moonshine, with birds and bowers—
One endless night of moonshine, love and flowers.

" Bright was the morn, and sweet the pibroch's strain
That filled my high palace and filled the plain,
When chaste Lucina a lovely boy did bring,
A royal prince, to be the future king.
The pious monk that dwelt in cloistered cell
Came forth that morn the joyous crowd to swell;
My halls were thronged with valiant knights in mail.
And lords and ladies from the quiet vale.
Grand was the feast—the wine did sparkle bright:
Grand was the feast that ended not with night;

Three days and nights the festal board was spread,
And every hall resounded 'neath the tread
Of hooded monk, gay lord or soldier bold,
And minion, whose base love is bought with gold.

" Like some proud bird that soars to realms on high,
Scorns the base earth and seeks the distant sky,
When borne aloft on self-sustaining wings
Far from the sight of sublunary things,
He sees beyond him worlds as bright as this—
Worlds without number—worlds as full of bliss;
I looked upon the proud and happy throng,
Whose life seemed sweet, like minstrels' dulcet song;
I thought myself the source from which did spring
The constant pleasures of a potent king.

" Ere twelve revolving silvery orbs of night
Had waxed and waned, and shed their mellow light,
My royal spouse, inflamed with venal love,
(Unlike the pure who dwell in Heaven above,)
Forsook a monarch's couch and festal board
For one who loved her not—a base-born lord.
One night I missed her from my royal side—
I missed my high-born, foreign, beauteous bride,
And stealing out at midnight's solemn hour,
I found her seated in the rosy bower,
And listening to the love and plaintive tale
More sweet to her than song of nightingale.
I rushed upon the proud and guilty pair
And sent them to the depths of black despair.

" My heart grew sick, my brain grew fierce and wild—
I rushed to the palace and seized my child—
I seized thee, Estell, with these bloody hands,
Left my rich realm and fled to foreign lands.
Behold your father, Estell, yet I trust
My sins are all forgiven; with the just
I long to dwell in that bright world above,
Where all is peace and all celestial love.
Take this full purse and take this signet ring—

Nay, start not, boy; wert thou not born a king?
Thy father once was mighty; his renown
Is yet revered; take, then, the regal crown.
These are the treasures I have saved for thee ;
Then sail ye hence o'er the dark blue sea—
Haste to thy father's throne, where willing hands
Of trusty subjects will restore thy lands.
Mine hour is come ; th' insatiate monster, Death,
Is here. Soon will this fleeting, mortal breath
Have ceased. Come closer, now, 'tis cold, my child—
1 see thee not—'Thus died the hermit wild.

"If you think this poem contains any merit, I have
no objection to your showing it to dominie Heflin.   In
a few days you may expect to see Corie and your

FALKNER."

CHAPTER XXV.

MR. MANNING made extensive preparations for the reception of the boys. He intended that they should be taken by surprise. He did what Southerners are ever apt to do upon extra occasions—*killed a pig* and barbecued it. (You need not laugh, reader, your father did the same thing when you were expected home!)— Mrs. Manning sacrificed a fat gobler at the altar of maternal love, and a real festal board was spread for the boys.

The family carriage was dispatched to the town to receive the boys at the station. The good Mr. Manning delivered his *proclamation* and the servants rejoiced in a holiday.

"Come, Dick," said black Joe, "lets dress up in our best bib and tucker, as aunt Phillis calls it, and go and meet mos Falkner and massa Corie. I tell you, mun, if you don't put on good close, and wash dat black skin o' yourn, massa Corrie will get out de carriage and comb your head for you. You know how he combs heads, boy. He jes takes de curry comb and 'pears like it does him good to hear you holler."

"Dat is all true, nigger," said Dick, "but den as ole moster's already gin me to mos Corie, I don't care much cf he does sorter whip me sometimes. He gi's me many

more things den mos Falkner does you. Mos Corie's
got too much sense dan hurt his nigger; he jes makes
out like he hurts when he dont."

"Now, Dick," said Joe, "you never seed mos Falkner hit one de black foax in your life. I don't know
dat he ever expects to. I jes bleeve he gwine make a
preccher. I hope mos Falkner giv me sebenpens. I
don't 'spect *your* moster got any, 'cause he ollers spens
his munny jes for foolishness."

Those negro boys, whom the father had given to his
sons, (as all farmers do, simply for the sake of letting
their children have something to claim,) chatted away
as happily as if they expected their young masters to
bring them a fortune. Fully two hours before the carriage was expected, Joe and Dick started off in a sweep-
ing trot to meet it. When they had proceeded about
three miles at that rapid rate, they espied the carriage
moving slowly down the hill. They increased their speed
and rushed forward to meet the carriage, hallooing all
the time, "yonder cums mos Falkner—yonder cums
mos Corie! bless God! dis nigger want to die; get out
de way and let dis nigger run. Black Sam think him
self mity smart settin' up dar drivin' dem fine college
boys."

"Howdy, mos Falkner—howdy mos Corie; how you
boaf bin dis long time?"

After the familiar salutations had been passed, Corolan ordered the driver to stop. He opened the door,
alighted from the carriage, and walked up to Dick to
compare hights. Having satisfied himself that black

Dick had outgrown him, Corolan mounted upon the back of the stout negro, as he had done a thousand times before, and rode him in advance of the fast trotting horses fully a quarter of a mile before Dick could be prevailed upon to let his precious rider dismount. When Corie dismounted, he made Dick perform several evolutions, such as turning summersaults, jumping up and striking his heels together three times before he touched the ground.

"Now, mos Corie, gin me one quarter dollar, plees sir; you know you promused me one if I would take good care ob de black pony, and keep de tother niggers from trublin' de fishin'-poles when de white foax gone to church ebry Sunday. Now, mos Corie, you nose you my moster, 'cause old moster gib me to you when we little childon, long 'go as I can 'member."

"Oh! you black imp," said Corolan, "I am glad I have something to whip you for; I have whipped but one negro since I saw your black skin last, and that was the boy that waited upon me at college. How often have I told you not to appear before me with your head half combed."

Here Corolan gave Dick a few light strokes with a switch by way of asserting his superiority, and drawing forth a horn comb from his pocket, the mischievous boy gave Dick's head a radical combing.

"Lord a messy, mos Corie, you pull all de har out po nigger hed. What you gwine do for nigger when Dick ded?"

"There is no danger of killing you, you ebony imp.

What good does it do me to have a negro, if I do not whip him at least once a year? You had no business being a negro, but since you could not help it, take this quarter and this handkerchief and cut out home. If you do not have the black pony curried down slick when I get there, I will comb your head well for you."

Dick started in a run, as happy as a king. He declared to Joe, who had made a draft upon the liberality of Falkner for fifty cents, that master Corie was the best young man in the world. He soon forgot the head combing, but he did not fail to obey the commands of Corolan relative to the pony.

When the carriage arrived at the gate of Mr. Manning, the father and mother went out and gave them a very warm reception. The dinner was served up in splendid style—several of the neighbors being present —among them the meek dominie Heflin and the pompous doctor Gillis.

CHAPTER XXVI.

It is not prudent to dwell too long upon one theme. We have given a faithful history of the lives of Falkner and Corolan from their childhood up to the close of their first year in the University and Preparatory school. Mr. Manning was so well pleased at the manly course and studious habits of the good Falkner, and so much surprised at the improvement in Corolan, that he shed tears of joy. There was only one thing wanting to complete his happiness, and that was an impossibility. If Falkner had been born his son he could not have loved him more than he now did; or even if it were possible for him to conceal from him the fact of his being a foundling, his joy might still be complete. Mr. Manning had a strange presentiment that Falkner would be exposed to perils, though he was confident that the boy had nerve sufficient to encounter any dangers that might beset him. If the feelings of Mr. Manning had been otherwise than of the most fraternal character, the doubtful parentage of his foster son would not have cast a darkening shadow upon his own manly brow.

He considered Falkner, whose hight was nearly equal to his own, as one of the noblest specimens of youth he had ever seen. His naturally effeminate face had lost a slight degree of its delicacy and put on the ruddy

visage of early manhood. His hair had assumed a
darker hue, yet the auburn ringlets' still clustered in
many a natural curl about his well-shaped head. His
eyes, as blue as the welkin, were not the least attractive feature of this interesting youth. Mr. Manning observed that Corolan had grown much, and his
face was gradually improving in appearance. Corolan
had been at home only a few days, when he expressed
a desire to return to school. It is strange, thought his
father, that Corie, who has never been known to love
school, should have improved so much as to desire to
leave home again in a few days, after having been absent one whole year.

"How is this, Falkner; has Corolan really a love for
books?"

"I think not, father," said the boy, "but brother is
improving rapidly; yet I scarcely know how he learns,
unless it is from the frequent drillings I give him nightly
upon his lessons, very much against his own inclination."

"You are a good tutor, my son; I had almost arrived at the conclusion that Corolan would ever remain
totally ignorant of the contents of books."

"I hope, father, that you will permit him to return
to the University with me. He may improve wonderfully during next year. If he remains at home he will
as surely spend all his time in riding, hunting and fishing as the means are placed in his power."

"You shall be gratified, my boy, and Corie shall be
placed entirely under your control. But, to change the

subject, why did you not relate how the hermit disposed of Estell when he left the palace so precipitately after the murder of the queen and her paramour?"

"I thought I would merely give the story a slight touch of romance, leaving your imagination to supply any defect in the narrative. I did not even give the name of the king nor denominate the country he ruled. The king's name was Bohomathalzal, quite an unpoetic appellation, as you will observe, and it was so difficult for me to insert it in the verse. I was fearful that Bohomathalzal might be a hard name to rhyme to, and I thought I would serve it like you do the gar fish when we are seining—throw it out. The name of his kingdom is Utopia."

"You surely mean Ethiopia, Falkner, as there is no such a country upon the map as Utopia. Probably you have been reading the Arabian Nights and have gathered some of your ideas from some of the strange fables you find recorded there."

"You talk as if you had not read the book to me and Corie when we were children. Do you remember how we used to laugh and clap our hands when you read one that was uncommonly interesting? But the 'Hermit's Tale' is strictly original with me, and was written merely to gratify a whim, at odd times. King Bohomathalzal received the crown from his father Anakthalzer, and was supposed to have been the most wealthy prince that ever reigned in Utopia. He gave his father's fine palace to one of his subjects and built another, which was the wonder of the world. Kings and princes came from distant countries to see the magnificent pile and to taste the rich dainties of his magnificently spread board. One of the kings of the East was so much delighted with Bohomathalzal that he gave him his daughter in marriage, whose dowry was forty millions of piastres. Bohomathalzal was so enamored with his queen that he expended thousands of dollars upon her wardrobe daily. Her beauty and rare accomplishments were so attractive that the premier of the king, who possessed as many graces of person and mind as the renowned Leicester, won her love and despoiled her of her virtue. The king loved her too dearly to accuse her, from silly reports and suspicions, but he could not withhold his hands from shedding blood when he saw his wife, at the dead hour of night, in social converse with his premier. He shot both of them dead and hastened to the palace, took a large quantity of gold and valuables, not neglecting the golden crown, and going to the bed of the royal babe, he took it up softly and carried it away with him. He was accompanied by a trusty servant, upon whom he enjoined secrecy. They traveled as private citizens, and took up their residence in a strange country. The self-exiled king bought a few roods of land and lived secluded with his servant and babe about two years. The servant was a white man, of rare intelligence, who had been a faithful attendant of the king's father. Bohomathalzal exacted a pledge from his faithful Adoniram, that he would never reveal his secret, but raise and educate Estell as his own son. He gave Adoniram a large quantity of gold, and taking his crown and jewels, and a few clothes, he went to another strange country and dwelt in the cell in which Estell found him."

"That is a very strange little romance of itself," said his father; "but you have not related any of the particulars of Estell's life."

"Estell," resumed Falkner, "was a very wild and venturesome boy. When Adoniram was not instructing him in the languages, the royal boy would stray from the cottage and engage in the sports of the chase. Upon several occasions he was wounded by the wild boars and panthers which he killed. He was not contented to dwell in that secluded spot, and tried to obtain the consent of Adoniram for him to join the army; but the good old man, who was noted for integrity, implored his boy to remain with him. Estell was hunting one day in the forest, when he encountered a sybil, who examined his palm and told him that he was the son of a king, and would see his father within a few years. He predicted that he would be a prosperous and happy monarch, but as the lines in his hands crossed so strangely, he would encounter many difficulties before he obtained the kingdom of his fathers.

"Estell related the sayings of the sybil to Adoniram when he returned home. The old man said to him that he had but little to do to listen to the tale of a wandering witch. But the boy, who had almost arrived at the age of manhood, allowed the prophecies of the sybil to prey upon his mind. He longed to be a great man. He had not the modesty of Moses, who refused to be called the son of Pharaoh's daughter, even though a crown should be placed upon his head.

"He could not, he would not remain in solitude. He threatened to throw himself from a precipice if Adoniram should not consent for him to go to the wars. The old man consented, and placing a fine steed at his disposal, invoked the blessings of the Virgin upon the head of the erring boy. Estell rode from the cottage as happy as a belted knight, not doubting the prophecies of the sybil. He lifted his mace and battle-ax and slew many imaginary foes ere he had ridden a furlong from the cottage of the weeping Adoniram. The fiery youth had all the beauty of Adonis and the valor of Achilles. He was received in the army, was among the foremost when a charge was to be made, was knighted, honored and rewarded by the prince whom he served.

"I have not yet seen my father," said Estell; "yet I have encountered many difficulties. Surely the words of the sybil are true.

"He was acting in the capacity of a spy upon the night he so strangely encountered his father in the person of the hermit."

"You have not told me, Falkner, whether Estell ever gained his kingdom."

"You must be interested, father, in my tale; you will not even give me time to breathe, before you hurry me on with the recitation. When Bohomathalzal died, Estell discovered among his relicts several letters which the hermit had written, directed to Adoniram, giving him directions as to his future course. Estell could not doubt but that the hermit was his father. The crown and royal robes were found in the cell. He had his father's remains transported to Utopia and interred in the royal cemetery."

"You are rather fast with your narrative, my son; you have not told me anything about the difficulties that Estell encountered in obtaining his kingdom."

"As to that, father, it is a long story; but if you will give me your attention after tea, I will relate all the particulars."

CHAPTER XXVII.

"Now, Falkner," said his father, when they had risen from the supper-table, "you must tell me how Estell obtained his kingdom."

"You may doubt the truth of some of my assertions, my dear father, but they are as true as some of the adventures which we read of in the Arabian Nights. The unhappy Estell had as many difficulties and dangers to encounter as Æneas of old experienced ere he arrived at the place of his destination. Often the shades of his father appeared to him in his dreams and implored him to bury his body in that strange land and hasten on to his beloved Utopia; but the good boy had taken upon himself a vow to suffer death before he would yield up the corpse of the deceased king. He was wrecked upon an island, where he remained with a few friends for two years. One day while they were out searching for drift wood, and eggs which were deposited upon the island by the sea-birds, they espied a vessel. With joy they discovered that the ship was making for the island. They were horror stricken when they discovered that the vessel carried a black flag at the mast head. The pirates landed and took possession of the persons and property of the unfortunate sojourners. Happy it was for them that they were able bodied men, or they might

have been slain. They were marched aboard of the
vessel and carried to a distant port and sold into slavery. It was fortunate for Estell that he had concealed
his treasures in a cave upon the island. He had buried
the coffer that contained the remains of his father.

"The master of Estell was a good man, and treated
him with much kindness. He was employed as an
amanuensis and interpreter, (thanks to the instructions
he had received from the learned Adoniram.) The
merchant died after many years, bequeathing his whole
estate to Estell, who had married his only daughter.—
Estell purchased a ship, sailed to the island, and placing
his treasures aboard, steered for Utopia, many hundred
miles away to the South. He had not revealed to any
person on board that he was the son of the late Bohomathalzal, trusting to Fate to solve the great enigma
of his strange life. When the vessel of Estell had proceeded a few hundred miles upon the expedition, the
ship of a pirate hove in sight. Estell gave the piratical ship a few broadsides, and fastening the grappling
irons to its sides, boarded it, followed by the trusty
crew. All the pirates except the captain were slain—
he being taken alive. What was the joy of Estell at re-
cognizing in him the pirate who had sold him into slavery.
He was immediately run up to the yard-arm amid the
shouts of the exultant crew. Groans were heard issuing from the cabin of the pirate's vessel. Estell went
immediately to relieve the unfortunate persons. Adoniram, the aged foster-father of the boy, was among the
number. He was released, and fainted in the arms of

Estell, whom he recognized. He had traversed half of
the globe searching for the adventurous boy. The vessel of the pirates was made fast to the ship of Estell,
and, buoyant with hope, the modern Æneas steered
again for Utopia.

"When the prosperous winds wafted them into the port
of the principal city of his kingdom, Estell was surprised at the magnificence of the buildings. He was
greeted as a stranger whose prowess had subdued the
wizzard of the seas. He had the difficulties of Ulysses
to encounter ere he obtained his kingdom.

"He learned that a foreign prince ruled in the place
of his father, and had brought over as many followers
of his own as William of Normandy conveyed to England. He had distributed the principal offices among
them—thus Utopia was held in complete subjection.—
He presented himself before the people and claimed to
be the lost prince. Adoniram, who was present, was
recognized by his old associates, and the story of Estell
was believed by many; yet, others, among them the
king, believed it to be a fabrication. The king issued
a warrant for the arrest of Estell, but he collected many
soldiers who were not well disposed to the usurper, and
resisted the authority of the pseudo king. The armies
fought long and desperately, and victory perched upon
the standard of Estell. The aged Adoniram brought
forth the crown which had been piously kept by Estell,
and placed it upon the head of his foster son. The
joy of Adoniram was so great when the king marched
into the palace, that he expired."

When Falkner had finished the narrative, his father was satisfied that the boy had more imagination than he had given him credit for. He cautioned the boy from indulging too freely in novel reading, but recommended a few standard works for his perusal.

Within a few weeks Falkner and Corie bade farewell to the parents and departed for the University, very much to the gratification of the latter, who was dying to see his dulcinea.

CHAPTER XXVIII.

[FROM THE JOURNAL OF FALKNER MANNING.]

"TEN years have passed since I entered the University of M——. Ten years have passed swiftly away, yet they have been mingled with sunshine and shadow, love and grief, hope and despair. I try to be calm as I write, yet my mind is so troubled at the recollection of the past, I shudder to record my thoughts upon this stainless sheet. I would long to die, but it is sinful in me to wish to hurry myself into the presence of my Maker. I have learned ALL that Mr. Manning knows about my abduction, yet not enough to establish my parentage. How I long to see him whom I so dearly love! him whom I supposed was my father! And Corolan! these eyes may never again behold him, but I shall pray for him till life's last sun shall set.

"But let me be more explicit, and chronicle some of the principle events of my life. Perhaps these pages may be exhibited to the world when I shall have ceased to exist; perhaps my mind may be calmed by becoming familiar again with events which have nearly escaped my memory. If we do not *delight* to do so, we are forced to dwell upon occurrences of an unhappy nature.

15

"How happy was I when I joined the Sophomore class of the University of M——! Corolan was my constant companion, and from my kindness to him, he had learned to love and respect me. His mind reacted under my tutelage, and his reason, which was not obtuse except upon abstruse and scientific subjects, was suddenly loosened from the leaden fetters which bound it. He became as famous for his excellence in learning as he had formerly been noted for his inattention to books. Father—yes, I must call him father still—was not happier on account of this sudden change in the mind of Corolan than I was. He could scarcely believe his eyes when he opened and read the first letter Corolan had ever written. When father was assured by me that the letter had been composed by Corolan, without my assistance, he wrote me a long, loving epistle, entreating me to continue my laudable course of instruction. I was directed by him to allow Corolan as much money as he wanted, not doubting but that the boy had become as economical as myself. I did not reveal this to Corie, fearful that he might take advantage of it and relax again into indolent habits. I gave him whatever I thought he needed, not refusing anything within the bounds of reason that he desired. His love for me increased, and I joyfully perceived that he would be able to enter the University by another year. How quickly that time rolled around and found us again at the University! As I had expected, Corolan applied for, and obtained an entry into the Freshman class. I rose Junior, having maintained the first position in the two lower classes. Father was so overjoyed at the success of Corie, that he insisted upon paying us a visit. He went to the College and spent one week with us. That week was one of the happiest of my life. I had a bed prepared for him in my room. One night during his visit, I waked up and saw father bending over me, weeping bitterly. He bedewed my cheeks with his tears. I asked him why he grieved; he could give me no answer, but, bending over me, kissed me more than once and retired to his bed. I could not divine the cause of his grief, thinking that he was sad on account of being about to leave his children so soon. I can now divine the cause, oh! father, but then I thought I was your own son.

"Father left us, having made us many fine presents, and enjoining upon us to write to him every week. He embraced Corolan more tenderly than he had ever done before, but when he came to take leave of me, his frame shook; he pressed me to his bosom, he kissed me, and tears, which he could not restrain, flowed from his eyes like rain-drops. How I remember his looks on that morning! His finely-formed, handsome face looked sad and sorrowful. I had never discovered before that his hair had commenced turning gray. His mild and beautiful eye seemed a little sunken. I supposed that he was unwell. No, it was sorrow; it was the visible trace of grief; it was dejection, on my account alone. He knew my nature so well that he feared to tell me I was a foundling. Bless his good heart! his letters are read by me with care and tenderness. If I should ever dis-

cover *my* father, I know I shall not, can not, love him
with half the ardor that I did (and do yet) Mr. Manning.   But I digress.

"Corolan maintained a fair standing in his class, as
some supposed, from my superior tuition; but it was not
from that cause.   His mind, naturally active, was as
capable of grasping a subject as mine, and he devoted
his whole time to his studies.   He had an excellent
constitution, thanks to the superior training he received
from father in our field sports.   He was capable of performing heavier tasks than I could.   I remember that
he had set up several nights, on one occasion, in suc-
cession—during the whole of which time he never ceased from study.   His pride was fully aroused, and he
stood at the head of the class at the close of the Freshman year.

"He was successful in obtaining the love of his dulcinea, who promised to become his bride when he obtained his diploma.   She was indeed a prize.   Her beauty
was of that soft, dove-like kind that renders the Italian
ladies so charming.   I have never seen but one lady
who was her superior in point of beauty and accomplishments, and that was—yes I must name her—that
was my own flame, Elfrida Mordaunt.

"When the diplomas were distributed to the graduating class at the end of my fourth year in college, and
it was announced that I had obtained the first honor,
there was general applause.   As I went upon the ros-
trum to receive my diploma, I observed that father, who
was seated with the trustees, was weeping for joy.   I

received my diploma from the distinguished Mr. Rockford, who was appointed by the authorities to deliver the diplomas and the prizes. He is the same man who traveled with Corolan and me when we first went to the University. He was then in quest of a lost son. I remember every word he said as distinctly as if it were yesterday. He is the finest looking old man I have ever seen. When he delivered to me the diploma and the prize, I thought his voice and manner of speaking were unequaled. He pressed me warmly by the hand, and congratulated my father for having so talented a son. I long to see him again; but how could I meet him, now that he is the Governor of the State and I a poor artist? He is the guardian of Elfrida, whose love I sought and obtained when I was in the senior class. She was placed at the Female College of M—— by him, where she graduated with honor.

"I returned home with father and Corolan, who was as loth to part with his affianced as I was sorry to see Elfrida depart with her father for Crofton. I promised Elfrida, before I left, that I would come to Crofton when one year had passed. I had not sought to obtain Mr. Rockford's consent to our marriage, preferring to wait until we had tested our affections for each other thoroughly.

My father was duly informed of my intentions—for I had never kept an important secret from him in my life. He interposed no objections to my going to Crofton. Brother Corolan had gone back to College, leaving father and me to enjoy our sports alone. We spent the mornings in shooting ducks and partridges, and the evenings in reading from select books. I amused myself at times in drawing and painting. I had learned the art well. I painted the portraits of father, mother and Corolan, which were admired by all who saw the pictures.

"A few days before the time arrived for me to take my departure for Crofton to see my Elfrida, father—who had been long in conversation with mother—approached me, weeping, with a letter in his hand. He extended it to me and sorrowfully bade me read it. I did so and fainted in the arms of the good man. When I revived, mother was weeping bitterly and bathing my forehead with cologne.

CHAPTER XXIX.

[FROM FALKNER MANNING'S JOURNAL.]

" MY mother was standing over me, bathing my temples and administering what remedies were at hand.—When I opened my eyes, my memory revived, and I was the most wretched of mortals. A foundling— ' *Umbra nominis stat* '—all hope fled ; all the dreams of youth vanished. Elfrida lost to me forever ! Would she who had *engaged* herself to the son of one of the magnates of the land remain faithful to her pledge when she discovered that I was a foundling ? Was it **right** for me to deceive her, even though my reputed father should permit me to retain the name I had not **disgraced, and endow me with half his fortune ?** I could **not,** I would not deceive the pure being who might be made miserable. I may be the son of a low-born man, but the fine dress and the gold chain that were found upon my person gave a contradiction to that assertion. The letter that was enclosed in my wrapper gave no clue to my parentage. For the benefit of those who desire to learn something of the history of the unhappy man who writes these pages, the letter to which I refer may be read with interest :

"JUNE 4th, 18—.

"THEODORE MANNING, Esq.: You do not know me—yet I know you from reputation. When you discover the beautiful boy asleep at your door, receive him as a gift from Heaven. You may learn something of his history in the future—but not now. That he is one of the most beautiful boys you ever beheld, there can not be a doubt. You have just lost one about his age, and it may not be improper for you to adopt him. You are soon to remove to another portion of the State, and it will not be inconvenient for you to adopt the boy as your own son. If you make any publication of the discovery of a foundling until the injunction of secrecy is removed from you, the boy will be slain, or yourself will be the sufferer in person. You may learn every thing relative to the child at some future day—but you *must observe secrecy.*   With respect,

"C. R."

———

Thus had my reputed father been held in suspense. Thus had my fates been balanced, as it were, upon a hair. I had been beset with dangers, yet my dear father and mother had carefully preserved my secret. The servants, who loved me dearly, had obeyed the commands of my father, who, removing to the place where I was raised, within a very few days after I had been *found,* easily persuaded the curious that I was his eldest child. I was but three years of age when I was stolen from my parents, and know nothing of my earlier history. The first thing I remember, was my standing by my mother's lap playing with brother Corolan, who was then an interesting child of two years of age. I was then about five years old. Corolan was a warrior from his birth. He commenced fighting me before he could pronounce my name. I have scratches upon my face, the marks of which will never be effaced until this flesh shall return to its original elements. It seemed natural for him to fight everything that moved. He is a stranger to fear, when his passions are excited. I never returned one of his blows, because father and mother taught me to love him and them.

"My father was so kind to me that I was unhappy when he went from home and remained beyond his usual time. Mother loved me dearly, but I could discern, without complaining, that she doated upon Corolan. I murmured not; no discontent was ever heard to come from me. She performed her duty, and I love her dearly, and shall honor her until the grave closes over her. Father loved me more than he did Corolan, because I almost worshipped him. Who could have helped loving so good a man as Theodore Manning! He was a model man, who concentrated all the happiness of this life around his own fireside. All the unhappiness that I feel is from the fact that I am not his son." '

"When I recovered, father took me out to ride in the carriage. He used every means in his power to pacify me and make me content to live with him and be his son. He offered me an equal share with Corolan in his immense estate, but I could not accept it. I had learned that my father was living, yet I did not know what position in society he occupied. If he was a boot-black and possessed honor and integrity, I would rush into his arms. But the dread uncertainty of suspense, ah! that is the most galling of all hardships.

"I refused to remain with the man whom I loved so tenderly. I refused to share his fortune with Corolan. That generous boy, who had learned to love me, would have surrendered the half of his own claim rather than see me depart. But the boy was absent, and I should see him no more. Blessed Corolan! may thy life be not beset with the same misfortunes that have rendered your brother Falkner so unhappy!

"Mother implored me to remain and share the love she bore her own Corie. Father wept, and entreated me not to leave him. But how could I remain near one I loved so well, knowing that our relations had changed! No, I could not stay; I had no name, and I must win one. I knew I possessed some talent. I had borne off all the prizes and the first honor from forty boys who were contending for it with all their might. I could draw and paint, and, that failing, I might be an instructor of youth. The world owes me a *name* and a *living*, thought I to myself, and I WILL carve out my own fortune.

"Father made me promise to receive immediate assistance from him. I consented, but with a mental reservation."

Before I proceed farther with my narrative, I will place the letter of Rodman before the reader:

"Manning Hall, July 1st, 18—.

"Theodore Manning, Esq.—

"*Respected Sir:* The object of my writing this letter is to give you some information respecting the interesting boy you claim as your son. You have been kind to me, and Falkner has been to me as a ministering angel during my illness. He is not my son, but I hold the secret of his birth in my breast. I have an end to subserve, and his *own father* must learn the secret of his retreat from me alone. You love the boy, and it is well, or I could take him from you at any moment. He adores you, and I am contented for him to remain in ignorance of his birth until he has graduated. You may then tell him that he is a foundling, but if C—— R——can make it to his own interest, Falkner may be restored to his father. You need not endeavor to ferret out the father of Falkner. He can never discover his father except through me. If there is any advertisement inserted in the papers, Falkner may disappear.

"When the time, to which I have limited you, has expired, I shall be near Falkner; but until I can make it to my advantage, the secret shall remain within my breast.

"For the present I shall be known as

"C. Rodman."

CHAPTER XXX.

"I PROMISED to receive assistance from my father with the conditions that he would receive back the amount he might advance me when I should desire to return it. I was not long in making up my mind as to my future course. I resolved to go to Italy and take a thorough course of instruction under the chief masters of the art of painting, in the principal galleries of the most noted cities of that beautiful region. I thought, by adopting this course, my mind might be freed from the great burden of grief that was consuming my vitals. I had allowed my mind to dwell at great length upon Italy. I had read the works of Plutarch, Petrarch and Dante, and I desired to behold the everlasting city whose fame will exist through all time to come. Rome! Rome! what a world is spoken in that short word! Two thousand years ago it was the Capital of the World. Cæsar dwelt there in all his imperial pride; Cicero harangued the multitudes; the Scipios were renowned for their deeds of valor, and the Antonines gilded the imperial cities with their golden laws. I would see the ruins of the Colliseum; I would see the tombs of the Scipios, and stand upon the seven hills of the greatest city of ancient times.

"Yes, I resolved to visit Italy, the birth-place of the fine arts; the nurse of genius, if not the cradle of liberty."

"My preparations were soon made, and I bade adieu to my beloved foster parents. My father placed in my possession a check for one thousand dollars, upon one of the principal banking houses in the city of New York. He accompanied me to the nearest station, and I pressed his hand, returned his warm embrace and left him. I was strongly induced to go by the University of M—— and see Corolan; but how could I meet him! how could I part with him! My father must make the disclosure to him; I could not, I would not. His presence might baulk me in my purpose; I could notsee him. He never would have permitted me to leave him.

"I arrived at the great city of New York—a world in miniature, of itself. There were so many attractions in that city for one like myself, who had never traveled, that I was forced, against my will, to remain several weeks.

"When I embarked upon one of the principal vessels that made regular trips to Europe, I bade farewell, as I supposed, to my native land forever. I was in search of what I never expected to find—peace of mind. I was in search of a name—where should I find it? That was the main question.

"I left New York, the great Emporium of the Western World, to sail across the Atlantic. I cared not whether its waves should ever waft me back again; still, it was

not my intention to hasten my death. I longed to
hide myself in arid deserts. I longed to become familiar with wild scenes. But we cannot always shape out
our own course; we cannot ever direct our own bark.
The winds of prosperity or adversity may mock our efforts or may be propitious.

"I visited London, that great babel of the world. I
stood upon Tower Hill and wept over the fates of Raleigh, Wallace and More. Every place of note in that
great city was seen by me—some with indifference,
others with interest.

"I dwelt not long in the gay French Capital, but left
the minarets and towers of Paris with but few pangs of
regret.

"It was at Rome that I lingered; it was in the galleries of art that I tarried. My brush and pencil were
put in requisition for weeks and months in copying the
great models of the distinguished masters.

"Venice, sweet, smiling city of the sea, why was it
not fated for me to dwell within thy neglected palaces
forever!

"ITALIA.

"The rustic muse was Virgil's pride.
 As on the shady ground he lay,
 With kids and lambkins by his side,
 To hear the rural shepherds play.

"Beneath the beech-tree's spreading shade
 The herdsmen gathered in a band;
Damœtas with Menalcas played—
 The sweetest bards in all the land.

" And when the oat-pipe's strain was heard,
　The rustic maid with nimble feet
Prolonged the dance ; the old ones cheered,
　And time passed by on wings so fleet.

" The board was spread with apples red,
　And chestnuts from the valleys gay,
And berries from the grassy bed,
　That ripen in the month of May.

" And then for drink, the rippling stream
　Supplied them from its crystal tide ;
The milk was crowned with golden cream,
　The shepherd's first and fondest pride.

" Beneath the beech-tree's spreading shade,
　Those feasts no more the shepherd greet :
No more the swains in each loved glade,
　On rustic pipe those strains repeat.

" No more the shepherd maid with sighs
　Repeats her love to gurgling rills ;
No more Italia's lovely skies
　Smile on her peerless vine-clad hills.

" No more the bard, in magic numbers,
　Sends greetings to his friends in Rome ;
Freedom lies in death's cold slumbers—
　The rustic bard hath now no home.

" The Vandals from the frozen North,
　With cohorts gathered far and wide,
With war's dread tramp did issue forth,
　And pitched their tents near Tiber's tide.

" Long waged the war, the struggle great ;
　Italia's best blood flowed in streams ;
The pillaged fanes and templed state
　Live only now in poet's dreams.

" Land of the sun, Italia grand,
　Where sleeps the pride of other days ?

Where slumber now that mighty band ?
Where dwell thy bards of tuneful lays ?

" Perhaps some youthful Cicero,
   With magic words upon his tongue,
May yet spring forth as once before
   When danger o'er his country hung.

" Italia ! once so brave, so grand,
   Awake ! throw off the galling chains !
Drive despots from thy sacred land,
   Which once rejoiced in Virgil's strains !

" Land of the mighty Cæsar's pride !
   How dear to me in youthful days !
How fond I loved thee ! yet I sighed—
   A despot ruled thy hills and braes.

" Where are all thy shining treasures
   Brought from the conquered nations far !
Where are all thy haunted pleasures
   That made thee an imperial star ?

" As sunset gilds the western sky,
   And spreads its halo o'er the world,
And sets that orb and bids good-bye,
   While darkness is around unfurled :

" Thus leaden shadows o'er that land
   Lie thickly dark, and broke the lute,
And, leveled low with torch and brand,
   Italia sleeps—her bards are mute.

" The Tiber, flushed with golden hue,
   Still pours its noble stream along ;
No laden vessels rise to view
   That echo with the victor's song.

" No trophies from the golden East
   Are wafted o'er the ocean blue;
No costly wines to cheer the feast
   Give welcome to the honest crew.

" Fair Venice smiles, but not with life;
　　The gondolier's sweet song is still;
　The harp is hushed; the drum and fife
　　Are heard from every vale and hill.

" Dead is Italia's ancient fame;
　　Her noble deeds live but in song;
　Extinguished is the brilliant flame
　　That lighted up her fanes so long.

" Land of the brave! awake once more!
　　Awake thy sons to deeds of fame!
　Their blood-red falchions steeped in gore
　　Can but restore thy ancient name.

" One thousand years have passed away,
　　And downward still thy course has been;
　Five hundred more, and yet decay
　　Will on thy ancient realms be seen.

" Thy mighty sons that made thee great
　　Are not revered by thy cold race;
　Their deeds were valiant, yet their fate
　　Was smothered by oblivion's trace.

" Land of the sun, farewell! but yet,
　　When future heroes rise to sight,
　Thy star, though not forever set,
　　Will shine in realms of ether bright.

" I tarried in Italy two long, sweet years, and left
it with regret; I knew not why. I knew not why I
wept at parting with any place; a prison were as acceptable to me as a palace.

16

CHAPTER XXXI.

[FROM FALKNER MANNING'S JOURNAL.]

"I SAID that it was with regret that I left Italy, where I spent so many happy hours in visiting the galleries of art. It is true, that the beautiful land of the sun possessed many charms for me; yet, I felt as if I were in search of something I could not find. I had rowed with the gondoliers of Venice, and listened to their sweet songs and romantic stories; had stood in the decayed palaces of the mighty Cæsars; had wandered by the banks of the Yellow Tiber; yet I could not, I did not, realize the dreams of my boyhood relative to that sainted land.

"Where does the enthusiasm of youth spring from? Italy. Where does the neophyte in the arts and sciences, poetry, eloquence and philosophy obtain his models? From the land that Brutus tried to redeem from servitude. Shall it be ever thus that the birth-place of literature is to remain in obscurity and ignorance? The very citizens of that once happy country have forgotten their ancient language. The most learned of them know not the many valiant deeds that their ancient ancestors enacted. The orchards and vineyards which once enriched the owners of the soil, have gone to premature decay. The instructions of the swan of Mantua have been forgotten and neglected. Cimmerian darkness broods over the land—despotism exerts its potent sway. Italy may never awake from her lethargy, but let us wait and hope.

"I stood upon the Alps, and heard the thunder roaring and saw the lightning flashing beneath my feet. I gathered the vernal flowers at the base of those famous elevations, and saw the snows and experienced the chilling blasts of a polar region upon their summit. The armies of Napoleon had passed those gorges; the feet of Byron, Shelley, Keats and Goldsmith had pressed those glaciers, and should I dare to tread where mortal had ever ventured? No; fear has never been to this bosom known, though I have ever been esteemed as a quiet and unobtrusive man. I climbed the summits of the Alps, where the Swiss cottager, accustomed ever to brave danger, durst not venture. I communed with the spirits of those whom I imagined had ventured upon the most dangerous places. If wizzards, witches or hobgoblins existed otherwise than in the fancy of nervous mortals, it would have been a source of pleasure for me to have welcomed the apparition. While standing upon one of the highest pinnacles in the world, why did I long to cast myself down? It surely arose not from a desire to imitate the actions of a Curtius or Manfred, but all men have a strange desire to jump from high places. I would particularly advise the nervous man not to venture upon high mountains: their desires may overcome their judgment.

"Did I desire to dwell upon that summit forever? Did I wish to exclude myself from the balance of my race, and end my days in those frozen and frightful solitudes? I know not, I care not. My feelings were not as they were when I read of those ærial regions. I crossed the beautiful lowland regions of *la belle* France, and my heart leaped afresh at the goodly sights I saw—a prosperous, happy people to all appearances. If their burdens were heavy, they repined not. The yoke of the despot seemed to sit lightly upon their necks. They sang to their tuneful harps, danced with light and merry hearts, trod the wine-presses, drank the health of their despotic rulers—yet they claim to be happy!

"I had learned to speak the French language with fluency at the University, but I could scarcely make myself intelligible to the Vendeeans. It is true, they were polite, clever and courteous; yet it is evident that they are only children of nature. France has changed her policy of Government so often, that it is impossible for the lower classes to keep pace with the strides of conquerors and rulers. It is certain that the tenets of the first Napoleon obtained a greater sway over that fickle people than the fixed laws of any king since the good times of Louis Quatorze.

"I passed into Spain. I wandered by the banks of the famous Guadelquiver. I listened for the sounds of a magic Æolian harp to strike upon mine ear—but I heard it not. The nymphs of poesy have even deserted those vine-clad groves. The Spanish maid hath truly hung her harp upon the willows, and its strings are all broken, and dead the sound. Yet, lovely Spain, the memories of the past will ever cluster around thee, and render thee, as ever, an interesting nation. That beautiful land of the sun rejoices in more natural advantages than its sister States—still the populace are an ignorrant, degraded, besotted race. But the grandees of Spain retain the pristine virtues of their ancient compeers. Some of them have yet the valor of the ancient Gauls—some of them could yet contend with another Wellington."

"Upon the deep waters of the dark blue sea again I embarked. As the noble ship cut the proud waves of the briny deep, I looked out upon that wild waste of waters and thought my life as cheerless as the prospect before me. The captain was a man who had passed the prime of life. He was tall and handsome, and withal very intelligent. He had been upon the sea nearly forty years. He might have been sixty years of age, still he might have passed for a man of middle age had not his head assumed a hoary garb. Captain Walsingham is a man whom to know is to love. His manners are mild, unassuming, and yet of the most fascinating character. He took a peculiar fancy to me before I had been aboard of the vessel one day. He said I had a striking resemblance to a charming little boy who was the child of Governor Rockford. He related the circumstance of his having given the boy a Newfoundland dog a great many years before, when the father and mother were upon a visit to his ship. It is very singular that I should be so interested in the fate of that boy, whom I, of course have never seen. I listened attentively to Captain Walsingham's narrative, and I could scarcely refrain from weeping when he had finished. I do wish I could see that lovely boy. I think they call him Sebastian. I wonder if he is as unhappy as I am? No, no, he cannot be; it is utterly impossible; no mortal knows how I suffer. But to return to Captain Walsingham. He seemed to love me. He praised my superior hight, extolled my music, and often when the sea was calm, and the sun was about to dip its fiery arc in the bosom of the distant waves, I would take my guitar, which I could at times strike in tuneful melody, and play for him some plaintive air. He had a fine voice, and sang delightfully. The tears would glisten in his eyes when I would happen to play a melody which revived the memories of the past.

"Captain Walsingham gave me a large Newfoundland dog, because I took a fancy to him. He said he would give a thousand such dogs if he could only behold Sebastian Rockford again. He has made his will, devising his whole estate to Sebastian, if he should ever be found. That boy must have been truly and wonderfully interesting and lovely. Walsingham was one of the first graduates of the University of M——. He seemed dearer to me for that reason. When shall I see him again? Bless his soul! he would receive not a *sous* for my passage from Madrid to S———."

"I am here in this dull town, fully one hundred miles

from father's residence. I long to go and throw myself in his arms, yet I cannot. Crofton is fully fifty miles lower down the river than this place. I have been here several months, yet have heard nothing from those I love. I will soon be out of money, yet I trust that the portraits I am painting may replenish my empty purse. I shall not stay here very long, but let come what may, I *must* go to Crofton and ascertain if Elfrida Mordaunt is yet single. But why should I care to know? She is the ward of the Governor and I am only a poor painter."

CHAPTER XXXII.

[FROM FALKNER MANNING'S JOURNAL.]

" THE night is dark, and my soul is sad. As I sit here in my lonely chamber and listen to the merry peals of laughter that come from the street below, my mind reverts to the scenes of my college days, when Corolan was with me; when we were happy; when only the faint shade of a shadow had crossed the path of my life. I feel sad; yet why should I repine? It may be that the darkest days of my life have passed. The curtain of Time may soon rise and present different scenes to my view. I have tasted of the bitter dregs of the cup of despair, yet the future may have bliss in store for me. If I could only discover my dear father, who has grieved for me so bitterly, I would bid sorrows depart, and fly to his arms. I would then go back to my foster father and ask his blessing. I love him too well to dwell near him, knowing that he is *not* my parent. Why did he not rear me as a foundling? I should not have repined if the discovery had been made to me at an earlier day.

"The only friend I have in this town is my Newfoundland dog. He is lying at the door of my chamber, guarding it from intrusion. Last night while I was asleep, I was aroused from my slumbers by his barking. In a few moments I heard the sound of a footstep upon the stairs. I apprehended no danger—feared none; the word is not to be found in my vocabulary. The hand that writes these lines can trace with delicate pencil, the softest tint of an oriental landscape, and hurl the bar and quoit farther than any man with whom I have ever contended. I feared no danger—had no enemy in the world that I knew of, yet the cautious tread of the intruder aroused my suspicions. In a moment after he had arrived at the head of the staircase, the dog disputed his approach to the door of my chamber. I rose quickly from my bed and sprang to the assistance of my noble guardian. As I opened the door, by the light of the moon I beheld a stalwart man, with long grisly beard and gray hair, standing to confront me. I asked the cause of the intrusion; he spoke not, but, taking a knife from his girdle, he rushed upon me. I seized his wrist, wrenched the knife from his hand, and hurled him down the steep stairway. Not desiring to return to a contest so unequal, the assassin left the house; I did not pursue him, but sought my room again. I lighted my lamp and examined the instrument of destruction. It is a beautiful dagger; the blade is of the finest Damascus steel; the handle is silver, inlaid with pearl. 'C. R.—to Ben Harley!' is the inscription. 'C. R.!' Was I so near danger without knowing it! Harley is the name of the wretch who desires to rob or slay me. 'C. R.!' Oh, how those horrid initials haunt me! Conrad Rodman, without a doubt, is engaged with desperate men. He is the one whom my kindness helped to restore to health. He stole me from my father. He is evidently near me; he alone can restore me to my birth-right. I will seek him out and denounce him. He shall reveal the secret, or I will plunge this knife into his bosom. I would rather die than be kept in suspense."

"I have seen Rodman, but for a few minutes. He is strangely altered. How differently he appears from the mild, gentle, intelligent man that gave me the chain! I seized him by the collar, held him fast, and confronted him with kidnapping me! I threatened to call the police and have him arrested. His hand sought a dagger that was concealed in his bosom. I hurled him to the ground, and was in the act of castigating him, when I beheld the same man whom I had encountered and disarmed at my chamber door. In an instant Rodman was gone, and I turned to grapple with my quondam stout antagonist. Thrice I hurled him to the ground, yet he returned to the attack. He drew a pistol and fired at me, but without effect. I disarmed and disabled him; he was at my mercy. I bade him depart, though I ought to have handed him over to the officers of the law. Happy it was for them, and unfortunate for me, that they engaged me upon the commons, or they would have been apprehended by the police."

"I have finished the portraits; my purse is filled with golden coin; I ought to be happy. I am going to

Crofton; 1 must see Elfrida, if but for a moment; I must gaze again upon her beautiful face, though she may be the bride of another man, whom Fate hath not doomed to despair, as it hath done me."

CHAPTER XXXIII.

[FROM MORTIMER ROCKFORD'S JOURNAL.]

"I HAVE lost my son; the light of the world is darkness to me. I am a man of sorrow and acquainted with grief. What is life to me, now that I have no Sebastian! My fine mansion and the wealth I have accumulated yield me no pleasure. It is true that my dear Josephine is left to me, but she is overwhelmed with sorrow. My hearth is desolate; the joy that lighted up my house has fled. Only twelve months have passed since his disappearance. I have reasons to believe that he lives, because I have received anonymous letters to that effect. I will start upon a tour of search for the boy to-morrow. The inhabitable globe shall be traversed or Sebastian shall be found. How bright and sweetly he smiled when I ordered the nurse to take him to the beach and see the wild waves dash against the shore! I knew not how much I loved him until he was lost to me and his dear mother."

"Five years have passed swiftly away, yet I have not found my dear son. I have been in every important city of the Union; have offered large sums for Sebastian, yet my heart is still bereaved. I suspect that

Royston has had something to do with his abduction. The police have discovered the robbers' retreat, and, as fate had directed, some of the ring-leaders have been discovered. Who would have believed that Hans Kremple and the painter Heinrich were implicated! It seems that they have been engaged actively with the band for a number of years. The police had been directed to the Hermit's retreat by some travelers who had barely escaped with their lives. The officers of the law concealed themselves in the vicinity of the den and witnessed the assassination of a man one night, and Hans and Heinrich were the principal murderers. They and Pierre, a French pirate, are now in jail awaiting their trial. I am engaged in the prosecution. Their trial will come on next week. The prison is guarded night and day, for fear of a rescue. Dame Elspeth and Dandie Doane were examined, but, nothing of a criminal nature being found against them, they were discharged. They have been forced to leave the country by the citizens, who have long suspected them.

"What a pity it is that Harley and the notorious Royston, who has been at large under sentence of death, should not have been taken!"

"I have just returned from the Court-house. The trial of Kremple, Heinrich and Pierre has terminated. There were many strange faces in the Court-house; some suppose that many of the confederates of that lawless gang were present. Kremple received the sentence of death with more composure than I imagined he possessed. Heinrich and Pierre were in a joyful glee when the Judge ordered them to rise and receive the sentence of death."

"A large concourse of people thronged the town to-day. I have never seen a greater crowd in the town of Crofton. The thoroughfares were crowded to overflowing at an early hour. When the jailor delivered Hans Kremple, Heinrich and the pirate Pierre into the custody of the Sheriff, the jolly crowd made the welkin ring with their cheers. Some of the boys asked Hans if he did not desire to sell them a patent for making saws, and teach them the art of erasing names from jewelry.

"While on his way to the place of execution, Hans stole the golden cross from the priest, and when he was swung off he held the purse of one of the by-standers between his thievish fingers! Heinrich and Pierre died sullenly, but there was much merriment over the *elevation* of the inimitable Hans Kremple. Hans would have made a safe companion to have taken a sea voyage with; for, as the poor fellow was surely born to be hanged, he might never have feared death by the waves."

"Twelve years have passed since the abduction of my sainted Sebastian. I have not yet despaired of seeing him again. We have adopted a lovely little girl of ten years of age. If Sebastian does not return she will be heir to my broad estate. I have lately been to the town of M—— to see Elfrida. I saw one of the most hand- some and amiable boys in the stage I ever beheld. He reminded me so much of my lost Sebastian, that I felt

a strange fondness for him. He said his name was
Falkner Manning, and his father lived at Oak-Lawn.
He had a little brother with him, over whom he was
exercising parental care. That boy will yet arrive at
distinction."

"I have just returned from the University of M——.
I delivered the diplomas and prizes to the graduating
class. It was with much pleasure that I conferred the
honor upon Falkner Manning. He is the most distinguished young man of my acquaintance. He bore his
honors so meekly, and reminded me so much of myself
when I was of his age, that had I not known that he
was the son of Theodore Manning, Esq., I would have
claimed him for Sebastian.

CHAPTER XXXIV.

[FROM THE JOURNAL OF MORTIMER ROCKFORD.]

"It is strange that I should have this load of sorrow to encumber me so long. I have grieved over the loss of Sebastian for more than twenty years, still I shed tears when I think of the beautiful face, the flowing auburn ringlets and the sparkling blue eyes of the beloved boy. I have hopes yet that my son may be restored to me, having received several letters of late from an anonymous author that Sebastian was living, totally unconscious of the names of his parents. It is strange that the individual who holds my secret within his breast should make no revelation to me.

"I have heard nothing from Royston for several years. He was recognized at one time and arrested. The officers who were conveying him to this place for the purpose of confining him in prison, were attacked by members of his desperate band, and the prisoner was rescued from custody.

"I firmly believe that Royston is the person that stole Sebastian, assisted by some of his lawless clan. Since the execution of Hans Kremple, I have called to mind the strange individual I saw with him on the evening Sebastian was abducted. I believe, now, that it was

Royston himself in disguise. If Royston desires a compromise, and will restore my son to me, he shall be rewarded with wealth. I am the Governor of the State, and will pardon him if a petition is presented from a respectable source."

"I have lately heard of the death of my aged aunt Margery. May the sod rest lightly upon her breast, and the flowers bloom sweetly around her sacred grave. Her fair daughters have made exemplary wives, (thanks to the good advice of their mother.) Mr. Watson and Mr. Judson were happy in their selection of partners. They have frequently visited me. The party I gave them when Sebastian was a child, will ever be remembered by me. They were so happy; we were all happy."

"There are some things I delight to remember; and as their scenes come up from the mist of long forgotten years, I put forth my hand to draw aside the curtain of memory, as if about to gaze upon a picture which once had the powers of fascination. Yet, I pause and reflect ere I draw aside the veil that divides me from the scenes of former years, as if I feared the change would produce disappointment. How often have I imagined that the house in which I passed the first years of my existence equalled in splendor some noble old Gothic structure, yet a visit to the old homestead, which is scarcely two miles from my own house, dispelled the illusion. It is strange I had not visited the house since the death of my father compelled my mother to leave it and dwell in a cheaper cottage. How changed, thought I, is the

17

scene; but still, time had dealt gently with the old house, and memory revealed every picture to my admiring gaze.

"In youth, our admiration of the most trivial objects is only equaled by the pleasure we experience during all those golden moments which come no more in after life. Our pleasures die as the flowers, but they live embalmed in our memory like some departed hope, which may return with the soft rays of Spring. Our tastes change; the flowers and birds that once delighted us, yield us no pleasure, because the associations which made them dear are far away.

"I stood beneath the tall oak, where my dear father used to sit, and, as I fancied I could see the good old man reclining in his easy chair beneath the umbrageous boughs of the graceful tree whose branches were the homes of the tuneful choristers, I brushed away the tears that voluntarily dimmed my eyes. I hope that I may meet my father again, in that better world, where parting is never known—where sorrows come not— where pain is felt not. Is it not a tender mercy, that Earth is not the abiding place of the saints, but that a holier and happier sphere is prepared for them by the wise Ruler of the Universe? Death is only the gate through which we must pass to reach that Elysian plain that is watered by the river of Life. How solemn it is to visit the family cemetery, and see the graves of departed friends! Yonder is the grave of a man who was interred when I was a lad. I remember how I shuddered and clung to the skirts of my mother's dress as the coffin was lowered into the deep and solemn grave, and I heard the rumbling sound of the fatal clod falling upon the frame-work of the vault. He had died in the spring time of life, having hastened his death by draughts from the wine cup. The old spring is down yonder, beneath the hill, surrounded with sycamore trees. It was a sacred spot in my boyhood's days, and the trysting place of many happy thoughts. If I had a pleasant book to read, it was thither I hastened. It was there that my mother used to sit and tell me of the joys of Heaven. Fifty years have fled since I stooped to imbibe the sweet waters of that old moss spring; but I must cease—my soul is sad."

"I know not why my mind dwells so much upon Falkner Manning, who received the first honor at the University of M——, six years since. I have learned that he has lately returned from a visit to the Old World, whither he had gone to copy the paintings of the masters of the Art. Captain Walsingham was here yesterday, and informed me that young Manning was a passenger in his vessel. Walsingham was so much delighted with him that he gave him a large Newfoundland dog, similar to the one he presented to Sebastian. Poor Carlo sleeps at the beach near the spot where his young master was stolen, and a plain marble slab marks his resting place. Jupe reposes by his side. How they loved Sebastian! they grieved at his loss seemingly as much as we did.

"My hair is perfectly gray; yet my form is erect.

and my features have not assumed the appearance of old age. Josephine looks young yet, though grief has depressed her spirits. Elfrida has been a faithful child, and a great source of comfort to my sorrow-stricken wife. I know not why she has never married. I sometimes think that she has refused so many opportunities of marrying from the love she entertains for Josephine and me. She says she never intends to leave us. Bless her soul! she lights up our benighted hearth, and consoles us, to a great extent, for our losses. I oftentimes think she loves Manning, yet she has never revealed the secret to me. She seems interested in him, and often joins me in extolling his merits. Josephine goes out upon the beach and casts many long and sorrowful glances upon the sea—indulging the vain hope that every home returning vessel may restore Sebastian to her arms."

"I have just returned from the seat of Government, having been called thither on official business. When my term of office expires, I shall not again be a candidate for re-election—as I am tired of public life, and am heartily disgusted with the fawning and flattery of office seekers. I shall retire to the privacy of my own peaceful home, and spend the remnant of my days in the shades of private life. The world is a theatre, upon whose stage are enacted many strange scenes. The curtain rises amid the cheers of the impatient audience: a tragedy is performed, and the idle and listless laugh when a chief is slain; the sentimental young man may shed tears at the pathetic passages of a comedy."

CHAPTER XXXV.

[FROM THE JOURNAL OF ELFRIDA MORDAUNT.]

"THE year has almost expired, and I shall soon see Falkner. I have not yet told Mr. Rockford that he was coming; I have never informed him I possessed any than feelings of friendship for Falkner. I went to Mrs. Rockford's room one morning for the purpose of making the *confession*, but my lips faltered, and my tongue was silent. Falkner will soon be here, and my cup of bliss will be full. I think he bears a striking resemblance to the portrait of the beautiful Sebastian that hangs in the parlor. His hair and eyes correspond exactly with Sebastian's, though the curls of Falkner may be a shade darker. Yes! yes! I am too happy! Falkner will bless my sight ere one more month shall have elapsed. His last letter was so full of love that I pressed it a thousand times to my lips. It is now in my bosom. where it shall remain until I see him. I have placed it next to my heart, which beats fond and fervently for him, and him only. I know he loves me tenderly; I know he is faithful and true to all his pledges. I love him the more tenderly because he loves me for myself alone. I told him that I had no fortune; that I should never consent to receive the estate that belongs to Sebastian, or any portion of it, as he might be restored to his father. Yes, he loves me for myself, and this faithful heart will cease to beat ere my love for him shall grow cold."

"Ah, me! I am so miserable! Fate hath decreed that I should be unhappy. All is dark and dreary; the future hath no bright hopes for me; the day no sunshine. I recall the lines of the poet of Nature to memory:

'Had we never loved so kindly,
Had we never loved so blindly.
Never met and never parted,
Then we'd not been broken-hearted.'

"I cannot blame him; I cannot reproach him; I cannot cease to love him. Oh! the fatal letter! it came this morning by post. It has plunged me in a sea of sorrow. The noble, generous Falkner is not less happy than his miserable Elfrida. How his heart must be troubled! how his mind must be tortured, to leave the good man whom he so fondly loves! He has released me from every obligation, but that is cruel; I would have loved him more tenderly for his misfortunes. Suppose he is a foundling, he is none the less noble—none the less dear to me for that. He is upon the broad waters of the ocean ere this, and is borne far away from her who adores him."

"Three years have passed since I saw Falkner—three long years, filled with bitterness. My secret has been kept within my own breast, and there it will remain forever. I cannot think he will ever return. He is so pure, so sensitive, so refined, that he wrongly imagines he is disgraced. He will never return, I fear; he will pass his life amid solitude; he will delight to remain in obscurity. If I could only see him; if I could only speak to him, it would lessen this burden of grief at my heart. No! no! I must pine in solitude. I must reject the addresses of every one as I did those of H——.

"Mr. Rockford has been elected Governor, and I am to go to the Capital to spend the winter during the session of the Legislature. Mr. Rockford looks so noble, and is so little elated at his distinguished honors, that I am astonished. He would give all his wealth to have Sebastian restored to him."

"I have just learned that Falkner has returned! he is near me! he is in Crofton! Shall I see him? Has he forgotten his Elfrida? No, never! never! If I knew that he loves me yet, an eternity of bliss would be centered in a moment.

"Be still, my throbbing heart, be still! Elfrida is *unhappy!* Elfrida is *happy!*

CHAPTER XXXVI.

[FROM FALKNER MANNING'S JOURNAL.]

"When I had resolved to go to Crofton, I commenced making preparations for the journey. My trunks were quickly packed, my bills paid, and I left the place, having hired conveyance and a driver. As we proceeded along the road that extends through the beautiful country, I was forcibly reminded of the home of my childhood, and I wept. My own beautiful land of the South is not less lovely than the most smiling portions of Italy or France. The leafy magnolias, which bear the sweetest flowers that ever bloomed; the stately pines, whose stalwart branches have withstood the storms of an hundred winters; the graceful sycamores and elms; the live-oaks and cypress, beautify those never-ending groves, while the vine, the lowly shrub and honeysuckle fill every place with flowers and fruits. Was the land of Beulah more lovely in the eyes of the Israelites than the beautiful vine-clad land of the South is to us? Mountain and valley, hill and plain, river, brook, spring and fountain present one continued round of beauty and interest. Who that is born at the South would care to dwell in the frozen regions of the North?

"It was nearly night, and the stately pines cast long

shadows across my path. I saw several men skulking behind the trees, endeavoring to shun observation. I directed the driver to be upon his guard, and force the horses to their utmost speed, if an attempt should be made to attack and rob us.

"I was not kept long in suspense. We had proceeded scarcely another mile on our journey, when a man, mounted upon a charger that had the appearance of having been ridden very hard, advanced to the carriage and ordered the driver not to proceed another step at the peril of his life. The robber wore a mask, but from his form and the appearance of his gray hair, which his hood failed to conceal, I easily recognized Harley, or the ruffian whom I had twice before encountered. I demanded of him the cause of my being thus rudely stopped upon the highway, at the same time ordering the postillion to drive on. The highwayman drew a pistol and discharged it at the head of the postillion, who, falling from the box a moment sooner than the report was heard, escaped with his life. I sprang from the carriage and went to the assistance of the cowardly fellow, who was nearly insensible from fear. He was trembling in every joint of his cowardly frame. When I raised him from the ground he could scarcely stand. Four men emerged from the woods and awaited the commands of the leader, who sat upon his horse, a cool spectator of the scene. I knew my own strength, and did not fear those who were directed by the leader to force me to submit. I drew out a pistol and fired it at the foremost man. He fell instantly, but I was closely pressed by the others, who were within arm's reach of me. I smote one of them with my heavy stick, which felled him to the ground. I had a desperate encounter with the remaining two, inflicting upon them several severe wounds with my knife. Two men rode up to my assistance and the graceless assassins fled, leaving behind them the robber whom I had shot. I was bleeding from several severe wounds I had received during the combat.

"I was glad to discover that the man was not dead. I placed him in the carriage and looked around for the postillion, who was lying at a little distance from us with his face to the ground. I raised him up, telling him there was no danger; he slowly recovered his senses and went back to his position on the box. I thanked those who had come to my assistance, and they accompanied me to the nearest house, where my wounds and those of the robber were dressed. The physicians said that the man was seriously, but not mortally, wounded.

"I was able next morning to proceed upon my journey, leaving the wounded man with the landlord, who promised to have him sent to Crofton for commitment as soon as expedient. I arrived at Crofton that evening, much fatigued, and feverish from loss of blood."

CHAPTER XXXVII.

"Father! Corie!" said Falkner, as he hastened to embrace Mr. Manning and Corolan, as they stepped into his studio, "welcome to my poor apartment. Is mother with you?"

Mr. Manning pressed Falkner to his bosom, and shed tears of joy. Corolan wept upon the neck of his beloved Falkner. It was long before they were sufficiently composed to reply to the interrogatories of the painter, who was just finishing a portrait of Governor Rockford.

"Falkner," said Mr. Manning, "you have been in Crofton nearly six months, yet you have not written one line to me. I was only made acquainted with your residence by accident. A traveler came to my house, and I gave him entertainment. He was very communicative, and I became interested in his conversation. I learned from him that he had witnessed the encounter between a young man by the name of Manning and several highwaymen. From his description, I was certain that it was my own self-exiled Falkner. He said that his companion assisted him in extricating you from a hazardous combat, though he was confident that you would have conquered them all. The man upon horseback had taken no part in the fight, from causes unknown to my informant. Corolan and myself made immediate preparations to come and see you.

"We were surprised to receive a visit from Rodman —whom you remember—on the day we had set apart to commence our journey. He is strangely altered, and time has not dealt gently with him. There is something mysterious about the man I cannot fathom. He said that the time had come for him to reveal the secret of your birth. He directed me to pack up the articles which were found with you, (when Heaven directed the person, as it seemed, to leave you at my room door,) and carry them with me. He could restore you to your parents beyond a doubt. He has not revealed the name of your father. Are you prepared to see him, Falkner?"

"I am," said the boy. "I would rather learn the name of my father, and rush into his arms—though he were the poorest man in the Universe—than remain in suspense. But whoever he is, I cannot, I shall not love him more than I do you. I have wronged you, my father, in not writing to you, but I could not."

"How you have grown, my son; you were tall, but rather slender, when you left upon your European tour. Now you are almost Herculean. Corie is scarcely half your size. Your form is similar to that of Governor Rockford."

"Father," said Falkner, "when shall I see Rodman? Did he tell you that I had encountered him and denounced him for his perfidy?"

"He is in town now, Falkner, but preferred stopping at an obscure hotel near the wharf. He would give me

no explanation of his preferring to take that course.—
To-morrow morning he will meet us in this room, where
the mystery will be cleared up."

Falkner had held Corolan in his strong arms during
the conversation with his father, as if he had been a
child.

Corolan was small of stature but had improved much
in appearance since last we saw him. He was slightly
below the medium height, though very strong for a man
of his size. His beard was long, and gave him a manly
appearance. Falkner was slightly above six feet in
height, and as finely-formed as the statue of Apollo.

"Falkner, my own brother—I shall never call you
by another name—you must return home and live with
us, and share our estate. You must never leave us
again. Put up the brush, throw away the paints, break
all the pencils, and go with us to the home of our happy
childhood. It was cruel in you to leave us and remain
away so long. My dearest wife will be so glad to welcome you. Mother is almost frantic to see you. I have
been married two years, Falkner. Our little boy bears
your name; do go with us and see him."

"I will go," said Falkner, "but I cannot promise to
remain. I will tell you my future plans after I have
seen Rodman. How is dominie Heflin?"

"He sleeps the sleep of death," said the father. "He
often spoke of you during his illness, and shed many
tears at your departure."

"Where is the chain Mr. Rodman gave you, brother?" said Corie.

"I have it still, Corie; but he shall receive it back when I see him. The ungrateful man is not worthy of respect; besides, he is a robber, or he would not have been an associate of Harley's. It is reported and believed here that Harley was among the number of those who were slain in a skirmish with the police a few weeks since."

The father and sons spent the whole day in conversation, and when they retired to their beds at the hotel it was late. They retired to dream, perhaps, of what the morrow might disclose.

The lamps were lighted in the stately mansion of Mr. Rockford. The reader is familiar with the place, and it needs no further description than we have given of it heretofore. The Governor was seated with his wife and Elfrida at the supper-table. Elfrida had just informed them that she was the affianced bride of Falkner Manning, the poor artist. The Governor said he would not withhold his consent. The conversation was broken off by a loud knock at the door. Mr. Rockford went to the door and beheld an aged and infirm man, who craved an audience with his excellency. He led the man into the library, and desired him to take a seat.

"You had a little son stolen from you about twenty-three years ago," said the man. "Have you heard from him of late years?"

"I have not," said Rockford, becoming interested.— "Pray keep me not in suspense. Tell me instantly, in the name of God, do you know aught of Sebastian? Speak, man, does he live?"

"He lives," said the man; "and you may see him soon, upon conditions. Do you remember one Carl Royston, who made his escape from prison on the night previous to the day set apart for his execution?"

"I do," said Rockford, "and I have long supposed that he was engaged in the abduction of the boy."

"He was," said the man. "He told me that he did it for revenge. He has seen the error of his ways.— The last one of his band has suffered death, and he alone remains. He cannot present himself before you except you will sign this instrument. When that is done he will conduct you to your son."

"The Governor took the instrument and examined it, (which was a form drawn up for the pardon of Carl Royston, under sentence of death for the murder of Jonathan Winslow.)

"I do not know whether I ought to sign this or not, sir. I am the Governor of the State, and Sebastian is my own son. I am willing to give this man Royston thousands of dollars if he will restore my son, but I ought not to sign his pardon. What is your name. old man? you look feeble."

Mr. Rockford ordered a glass of wine to be brought, and the old man drank it. He seemed much revived, and resumed the conversation.

"It may not interest you to learn my name. I came upon an errand of mercy. Royston will not receive your gold. If you do not sign the pardon you may never recover your son."

"When shall I see Sebastian if the pardon is signed?" said the excited Governor.

"To-morrow," said the man.

"Hand it to me," said the Governor; "I would do it were it the last act of my life."

The name of Mortimer Rockford was affixed to the instrument in an instant.

"But I must keep the pardon in my hands until I see the man Royston himself."

"You can have the opportunity to-night, sir," rejoin- the man.

"Then let us go instantly to him," said the Governor. "moments seem like hours to me."

"Royston stands before your excellency," said the man, who, pulling of his gray wig, and freeing himself from the long black wrapper, revealed the person of Conrad Rodman, or Carl Royston.

Morning came. The day was beautiful. The sun shone in splendor, and the house of the Governor was thronged, as usual, with early visitors. Rockford excus- ed himself, requesting his friends to remain with his wife and Elfrida. He and Royston (who had remained with him during the night) left the house and proceeded to the town.

"Let me step into the studio of the painter one mo- ment, Mr. Royston," said the Governor, "and I will at- tend you. He has been painting my portrait."

When Rockford entered the room of the artist, he was surprised to see two strangers with Falkner.

"Mr. Manning, I am glad to meet with you again; I scarcely recognized you. This is your younger son.

I have been surprised that your son Falkner, here,
should have taken it into his head to be a painter.—
Have you failed in business, sir, that Falkner was driven
to this expedient ? He informs me that he is penniless."

Mr. Manning looked sad, Falkner blushed, and Corolan was confounded.

"Your excellency will excuse me if I give you an
evasive answer," said the good farmer.

At that moment Royston, who had remained in the
street, entered.

"I have come according to appointment, Mr. Manning," said Rodman. "Falkner, I hope you will forgive me. I can repair every injury I have ever done
you."

"How is this, sir," said Rockford, "do you know
anything of this young man? Let us proceed upon our
expedition."

"I will soon explain, sir," said Royston, (or Rodman) this is the PLACE and this is the TIME to make the
revelation. Mr. Manning, you will please produce the
clothes of the boy"——

"What boy—what clothes !" said the excited Governor.

"The clothes of YOUR SON."

"Why should this gentleman have them ?" said the
Governor.

"Will your excellency please remain quiet a few minutes? I will soon explain every point."

When the clothes were unwrapped, and the gold chain

18

was held up to view, Mr. Rockford sprang forward and grasped them nervously.

"Sebastian's suit—Sebastian's chain! where is my boy?" said the Governor, as he fell to the floor. Falkner raised the stately form of the prostrate Rockford, and laid him upon his couch and bathed his head with water. When he revived, he implored Royston to conduct him to his son instantly.

"Falkner, behold your father! Mr. Rockford, receive back your stolen child!"

The Governor sprang from the couch and embraced Falkner with wild delight. Falkner could scarcely realize his happiness. Mr. Manning appeared as if in a dream. Corolan embraced Falkner and wept tears of joy. Mr. Manning related to Mr. Rockford all the particulars of the early history of Falkner, with which the reader is familiar.

"I have two fathers, now," said the artist. "My love for them shall be the same."

"We cannot stay here another moment," said the Governor. "We must hasten to mother, my own Sebastian. Come, my dear friend, Mr. Manning; come, Corolan, Royston, all. We must go and convey the news to Josephine."

They left the office of Sebastian (we shall call him by his own name) and proceeded to the house.

"I wonder why Mr. Rockford is bringing so many friends home with him? It is just like him—he often brings a dozen with him without having given me warning. Elfrida, do you see Mr. Manning with them?"

"I do," said the young lady; "and I must not remain here, but go and adjust my hair."

Mr. Rockford entered hastily, followed by Sebastian, who was the only one of the party that could keep pace with the lengthy strides of the excited and happy Governor, who, approaching the place where Mrs. Rockford was standing, said:

"Oh! Josephine, God has heard our prayer. Sebastian, behold your mother!"

We must let the curtain fall upon this scene.

Crofton has improved wonderfully since the abduction of Sebastian. Samuel Culverhouse and Dorothy have been sleeping for many years under the sod. Josephus Napoleon Bonaparte Snibbens married Miss Jerusha Smith. He named his first child Joachim Napoleon Murat Ney. He has not yet completed his knowledge of the classics, but it is hoped that he may do so before he dies.

There was a grand festival at the house of Mr. Rockford within a few weeks after Sebastian had been restored to his father. Captain Walsingham was there to give away the bride. Corolan and his wife and Mr. Manning and his wife were there.

All who were present declared that Sebastian and Elfrida were the finest couple that ever knelt at the altar.

ERRATA.

On page 73, for "*captivus fugivit*" read "*captivus fugit.*" On page 183, for "purest foundations" read "purest fountains."